HERNE BAY LIBRARY

Please return on or before the latest date above.
You can renew online at *www.kent.gov.uk/libs*
or by telephone 08458 247 200

I SHALL AVENGE!

When Kriso Tovak joins the Foreign Legion, he believes his beloved wife to be dead. However, discovering that she's still alive, Tovak deserts to join his wife in Prague. But he's captured, court-martialled and executed, which sparks a series of ghastly events in the Legion base at Dini Sadazi. And at the heart of it all is Annice Tovak, who takes terrible vengeance for the death of her husband . . .

Books by John Robb
in the Linford Mystery Library:

JAILBREAK
NO GOLD FOR TINA
FOUR CORPSES IN A MILLION
THE LAST DESERTER
THE BIG HEIST

JOHN ROBB

I SHALL AVENGE!

Complete and Unabridged

LINFORD
Leicester

First published in Great Britain

First Linford Edition
published 2011

British Library CIP Data

Robb, John.
　I shall avenge!. - - (Linford mystery library)
　1. Revenge- -Fiction. 2. Suspense fiction.
　3. Large type books.
　I. Title
　823.9′2–dc22

ISBN 978–1–4448–0854–4

Published by
F. A. Thorpe (Publishing)
Anstey, Leicestershire

Set by Words & Graphics Ltd.
Anstey, Leicestershire
Printed and bound in Great Britain by
T. J. International Ltd., Padstow, Cornwall

This book is printed on acid-free paper

1

The Execution

Twelve minutes to eight . . .

God, no! It was eleven minutes to eight. The clock hand had just moved.

Legionnaire Kriso Tovak made a wild calculation. He established that he had about six hundred seconds to live. A cigarette would last longer than that. So, if a man were to light a cigarette now — at this very moment — it would still be burning when he, Tovak, was dead.

Tovak whimpered. He pressed his terrified face still harder against the bars of his cell window. And he continued to stare at the big clock that brooded over the opposite side of the barracks.

Then he remembered that the clock always struck the hour. Just one reluctant, mournful stroke. *Clong* . . . Like that. Men new to Dini Sadazi often waited for it to go on chiming. But it never did. It was too old and it did not care. It had been there since the barracks were built and it had looked down on too much suffering.

So now that clock seemed to say: 'There — another hour has gone. But if you want to know which hour, you must look at me. I can't be bothered to talk . . . '

Would the firing squad take their time from that clock? Would the officer wait for it to strike before lowering his naked sword? And would he, the infamous Legionnaire Tovak, hear its grudging voice just once more before the Lebel slugs ripped life out of his quivering flesh?

Perhaps he would. The court martial sentence had been clear enough. The president had read it with the deliberate delicacy of a man savouring memorable prose.

' . . . At eight o'clock on the morning of Tuesday, June 19th, Legionnaire Tovak was to be shot until he was dead, in accordance with the provisions of the French Articles of War . . . his body was to be buried in the military cemetery at

2

Sadazi . . . his personal possessions were to be sent to his next of kin . . . '

Personal possessions! Tovak with personal possessions! It was absurd. Unless, of course, it was considered that a letter from Prague, eleven sous, two cigarette stubs and a photograph were worth bothering about. The letter, money and the stubs had been taken from him. But he had been allowed to keep the photograph.

Perhaps he had better look at it again. Just one last look.

He drew away from the window and the bars left deep imprints on his thin face, as though he had been branded. Tovak rubbed it with a twitching hand, then groped in his tunic breast pocket for the piece of pasteboard.

He could not hold it still. He had to lay it on the wood wall bunk. Then, to get a closer view, he knelt on the stone floor beside it.

Annice . . .

She was worth dying for. But it would be better to have lived.

Tovak's mind swirled backwards through time . . .

3

Back to the days when he and Annice had married in Prague. It was shortly before the hell of war had swept over Europe. They had been happy. Perhaps too happy. He had been a clerk in the offices of one of the city's many furniture firms. She — an expert in foreign languages — had been a translator for a shipping concern. And they had lived in respectable semi-comfort in a flat over a tobacco shop.

Until the jackboots arrived. Until the Teutonic tongue was suddenly to be heard everywhere in their ancient and lovely capital.

For a time, they had tried to carry on as usual. Tried to believe that the Germans would be driven away without any direct help from such humble people as Annice and Kriso Tovak.

But it was Annice who said in their flat one night: 'I've joined the Resistance.'

As simply as that.

He had been shocked, frightened. He had heard of the Resistance. Heard, too, of what the Nazis did when they captured members of it. He tried to argue with her. It was no use. Annice would never be turned from any purpose. And, he admitted, she was stronger and braver than he.

But he had joined, too.

He had been little more than a messenger.

But Annice had become an expert in explosives and sabotage. In such work a woman was less likely to be suspected than a man. And the cold indifference with which she could destroy life had sometimes horrified Kriso Tovak. Annice could hate as completely as she could love.

Ah yes, he had been in constant apprehension during those months.

It was not only for himself, but for Annice as well. The idea of the delicate and beautiful Annice falling into the hands of the Gestapo.

Then it had happened.

A party of black-uniformed men had called at their flat and taken her away. He had tried to stop them. He had thrown himself at them. But they had knocked him down and kicked him until he was unconscious. When he recovered, he was alone in the flat.

But not for long.

Later, they had called for him. And

they had sent him to Poland to sweat with forced labour gangs in the dry, brittle glare of the salt mines.

Somehow, he had survived. It was the will to see Annice again that kept him alive. He had never believed that she had been killed,

Never believed it until, the war over, he had returned to Prague. And there, after months of frantic enquiring, he found that Annice had been sent to a concentration camp. And, although no precise records had been found, it was almost certain she had been murdered.

So there it was.

Amid the debris of war, Tovak was alone. Annice was gone. His job was gone. And he did not want to stay in Prague. It held too many memories of her. Memories that were now a torture.

For two years he took any odd work that came his way. But always he was looking for a chance to get out of Prague. It was by chance that he heard some men talking about the Legion in a café. And he remembered all he had heard and read about it.

The Legion was an army for unwanted men, was it not? Well, Tovak was unwanted.

He made enquiries at the French consulate. Then to France — to the *Bureau de Recruitement*, in Rue St. Ouen, Rouen.

He went to Marseilles for initial training, after which he sailed with a detachment of recruits for Oran. This was followed by garrison duty in Algiers.

Finally, to this place. To Dini Sadazi. A stinking, sweltering cauldron, which served as an advance base for North Morocco.

And it was here in Sadazi that the letter had reached him.

The letter from Annice.

Annice had not died. But for two years she had been confined, with thousands of others, in a displaced persons camp. When at last she was free she had gone to Prague to find Tovak. And when she found out what had happened to him she went to the French consulate. It was with the help of the consulate that her letter had been forwarded to him.

She was waiting for him! Annice was in Prague!

He had to get to her.

And that was why he had deserted. It was his only hope. Yes, a ridiculously slender one, but better than no hope at all. And it had failed. Failed tragically. He had been arrested before he even got out of Sadazi. A town patrol had picked him up.

It was then that the madness gripped him. He had fought with his escort. Fought with the only weapon to hand, which was his knife. It was a sharp knife. And with it he had killed a legionnaire.

There could be only one penalty. The court martial had been no more than a tedious formality.

He had wanted to get it over — to end forever the bitterness and the misery. In more distant prospect, death had seemed desirable. But not now. Now that it was imminent.

Annice had enclosed the photograph with the letter and it had been taken recently.

Tovak put a shaking finger on it, trying to imagine that he was touching the living flesh.

She was still beautiful. Her flaxen hair

still fell to her shoulders, her eyes still had that level calm, her rich mouth still suggested unbroken courage.

He pushed the picture back into his tunic He did not want to look at it again, for it gave a twist of agony to his fear.

Back to the cell window.

Ten minutes to eight . . .

From somewhere in the distance he heard a few words of command and the steady thud of marching feet. But he could not see from whence it came. Perhaps it was his execution squad. They must have fallen in by now.

More feet. But these were closer and there were not so many of them. They were approaching along the stone corridor outside his cell. He turned and gazed at the door.

Another sound. This time, the slap of a hand against the magazine of a rifle. That would be the sentry sloping arms. A muffled voice. The door was being unlocked.

It seemed to open very slowly. In a half crouching position, Tovak pressed himself against the wall. For a moment, he could not see very well. Sweat had oozed from his forehead and on to his eyeballs. He blinked to clear them.

Captain Monclaire was standing in front of him. And behind the captain, two corporals.

The sight of his company officer made Tovak suddenly feel a little stronger, a little braver. Monclaire had that effect on men.

Monclaire said: 'Any requests, legionnaire?'

It was a formal question, spoken formally.

'None, *mon capitaine.*'

Tovak was surprised by his own voice. It sounded harsh and utterly unfamiliar. As though some strange and earthbound spirit had taken control of his vocal chords.

'No further letters?'

'I wrote my last letter yesterday, *mon capitaine.*'

That had been his letter to Annice. The letter, which had told her that they would never meet again.

Monclaire nodded. Then he said more

softly: 'Your time has come. It will be easier if you have courage. With courage, all things become easier . . . '

He hesitated, as if uncertain. It was unusual for the normally precise and confident Frenchman.

Then he added: 'There is a saying that cowards die many times in their lives. But the valiant taste of death but once. It may help just a little if you remember it.'

Tovak recalled the phrase. It emerged from among the dim and muddled memories of his schooldays. And perhaps it was true. How many times had he suffered all the terrors of death in this cell? Could the reality be as terrible as the anticipation? Probably not. Tovak felt something akin to courage start flowing through his veins.

He was almost glad when the two corporals fell in on each side of him and, with Monclaire leading, they marched out into the parade ground.

The sun was rising fast, but as yet it did no more than hint at the full heat of the day. The air had a clean sparkle. It reminded Tovak of the early summer in

Bohemia, when he had spent a holiday with Annice on the lush banks of the Elbe . . .

They moved towards the rifle range. It was there that all such business was transacted, with a human being serving as the target.

They were ready for him. Magnificently ready. Tovak found himself studying the preparations for his own end with real curiosity.

In front of the high wall, shielded with sandbags to a height of nine feet, a wood stake had been driven into the ground. Twenty paces from the stake the firing squad was assembled, with a lieutenant on the right flank. Tovak thought: 'They look worried and nervous. They don't want to kill me. Everyone is sorry for me. But no one can do anything about it because the military law says I must die.'

They halted facing the stake.

Monclaire made a signal with his hands. Tovak turned round. One of the corporals seized his wrists and strapped them to the wood. The other did the same with his ankles. The bonds were too tight.

But that, Tovak told himself, was only a temporary inconvenience.

He looked again at the firing squad. They were at the *repos* position and they were fingering the barrels of their Lebels uneasily. Those rifles had been loaded for them by the lieutenant — a single round in the breech of each, one of them a blank. Which was a pretty farce. A farce because it utterly failed in its object of making it impossible for any one of the eight men to know for certain that he had helped to kill. The theory was that each man could say to himself: 'I might have had the blank.'

But in fact any trained legionnaire knew the moment he squeezed the trigger whether he was firing a loaded cartridge. A blank had practically no recoil.

Tovak turned his attention to Monclaire. The captain was pulling a length of black linen from a side pocket. Tovak was glad of the darkness when it was wrapped round his eyes.

He was blind now. But his other senses were very much alive. He heard the retreating feet of Monclaire and the two corporals. Then he heard them stop after they had taken a dozen paces. He heard the lieutenant clear his throat. He heard the first command: *'Gare a vous!'*

Then the click of the squad coming to attention. Another order, and Tovak knew they had their Lebels pressed against their shoulders. They would be taking first pressure on the triggers and peering along the leaf sights.

Suddenly Tovak thought: 'I'm no longer afraid . . . I must be a brave man . . . '

Clong!

It was the clock. He had heard the clock again. The timing was good. But then the Legion always timed everything well. And he was glad he had been able to hear that mournful chime again. It was like a funeral toll. Very fitting.

He heard the last command clearly enough. And he thought: 'The lieutenant's voice is shaking,' He even heard the volley of the Lebels in the infinitesimal moment before he died . . .

2

The Woman

Evening in Sadazi. The eternal evening of Morocco. Stars so clear and so bright that a man feels he has only to stretch up to grasp them. The whole of the sky a diamond-clustered cloak. A cool breeze sweeping westwards from the blue mass of the Atlas Mountains.

The clock chimed over the barracks.

Clong!

It had sounded eleven times since the moment when Tovak heard it for the last time. Now Tovak lay in a shallow and undistinguished grave, amid many similar graves. But his story had not ended. Sometimes, by the single and inevitable act of dying, a man can start a chain of strange events. Events more important than anything for which he was responsible when he lived.

It was so with Tovak, the Czech.

15

And to follow them, we must leave the barracks. We strike north, walking through the small European area. Then into the much larger native quarter of the town. At first, the streets are comparatively wide. This is where the more prosperous Arabs live. But after a few minutes they narrow into mere alleys, bounded on either side by overhanging sandstone hovels and occasional cafés and wineshops. It is here that the legionnaires seek relaxation. It is here and in one of the wineshops that we must pause . . .

Legionnaire Rex Tyle held his glass of Algerian wine to the light. Then, as though facing grim duty, he put it to his lips.

The thin red liquid went down in a couple of swift and audible gulps. That done, Rex leaned his elbows on the table. There was an unaccustomed note of strain in his usually forthright American voice.

'I didn't like it, Pete,' he said to the broad shouldered, blond legionnaire who was sitting opposite him. 'It was no blank that was in my Lebel, and I don't go for killing a guy like Tovak.'

Pete Havers smiled without humour.

'You're not alone in that. I was in the firing squad, too. And I didn't have the blank, either. It was a filthy job, but it's best to forget about it.'

There was a touch of cynicism in Pete's cultured and very English tones.

Rex said: 'Hell . . . even a Limey can't forget a thing like that. Ain't you got no feelings?'

Rex tried to sound indignant, but he did not succeed. He knew that Pete's apparent indifference was no more than a projection of his natural reserve. And, in turn, Pete knew that Rex's more volatile personality was deeply upset by the macabre event of that morning.

They were opposites in many ways, those two. Yet they understood each other.

Pete understood the feeling of restless post-war frustration which had compelled Rex — an ex-G.I. from Brooklyn, New York — to seek a life of violent action in the Foreign Legion.

And, in a general way, Rex appreciated

why Pete had taken to the Legion after serving a short term of imprisonment in England for manslaughter.

A military and social code had then forced Pete to resign his commission in a famous English county regiment. But soldiering was his life. And the Legion was a natural refuge from the shambles of a smashed career.

A blending of two circumstances had brought them into the wineshop that evening. One of them was the fact that Rex had won a few francs in a lengthy and somewhat heated barrack-room card game. And Rex shared the usual American's view that money, once acquired, ought to be spent as rapidly as possible. The other was a desire to combat the depression they both felt following the execution of Tovak. Tovak had been in their company. They had liked the quiet little Czeck. They had been horrified when an evil chance of fate put both of them into the firing squad.

Rex refilled their glasses from a rapidly emptying bottle. And he talked on about Tovak. But gradually Pete's mind drifted.

And it embraced the memory of another man who had been killed. The man he, Pete, had killed. An elderly man, who had walked into his car . . . There had been no chance of avoiding him. But the verdict was manslaughter. The jury had been impressed by the fact that Pete had taken a few drinks before leaving the mess. And the sentence was six months' jail . . .

Pete lived it all again. Lines of strain seemed to etch themselves into his fine, almost delicate, features.

It was Rex who suddenly brought him out of the past and back into the present. Rex tapped his shoulder and said: 'Snap out of it, bud. You've just told me to forget. Now I'm telling you to do the same.'

Pete smiled.

'Sorry. I'll take my own advice.'

'I'm sure glad to know that. This party ain't exactly happy.'

They smiled at each other and raised their glasses. And simultaneously they saw the woman in the doorway.

Most of the other customers saw her,

too. The miscellany of legionnaires, Arabs and blacks, stopped drinking, smoking and talking to look at her.

It was not the fact that she was a European that caused the interest. Or the fact that she was well dressed. Or that her white linen frock emphasised the slim flow of her figure and the calm beauty of her face.

Women like her were not uncommon in Sadazi. They formed a big proportion of the more adventurous tourist parties, which came up from Oran. These tourists often visited the wineshops so that they could boast later of having been to a Legion advance base and slummed with real legionnaires.

And the legionnaires certainly had no objection to this. For such tourists usually entertained them to drinks and maybe handed them money.

She was alone. That was what caused the slightly astonished silence, which ended with a burst of gabbling discussion.

Very few tourists had the nerve or the stupidity to enter the native quarter alone, particularly at night. This lady was offering a persuasive invitation to robbery or worse.

She peered cautiously through the heavy, smoke-filled atmosphere, as though half hoping to see a familiar face. Then she gave an almost imperceptible shrug of her slim shoulders

Rex whistled long and softly. Then he whispered: 'What d'you know . . . ?'

'I know she'll find herself in a lot of trouble if she's not very lucky,' Pete said.

'Yeah. She's a sensation hunter, I guess. You often find the type among giddy blondes. I remember in . . . '

His reminiscence was cut drastically short.

The trouble had already arrived. A black Ashanti started it.

There were many Ashantis in Sadazi. Most were descendants of the Gold Coast natives who had been abducted and brought hundreds of miles north by the old-time Moroccan slave traders.

Generally, they were industrious and peaceable — except when drunk.

And this Ashanti was very drunk.

He was a big man, like most of his

people. His filthy, sweat-drenched European shirt was open to the waist, revealing an ebony black torso. It shimmered with strength.

The Ashanti put a huge hand on the woman's elbow and grinned at her. She tried to step back, but his grip held her. She tried to twist sideways, but he put out his other hand and steadied her with that. He said something to her which neither Rex nor Pete could catch amid the hubbub. But she coloured and made another effort to break away.

It was a ridiculous, futile attempt. Like a child trying to wrestle with a man. The Ashanti's grin widened and there was a gust of laughter from many of the customers. He let her writhe for a few seconds, enjoying a sense of primitive mastery. Then he pulled her to him and, without effort, slung her over his left shoulder. She tried to kick, but he held her legs below the knees. Her shoes clattered to the floor as the Ashanti turned and started to reel towards the table where he had been sitting with a couple of admiring Touareg Arabs.

Rex and Pete stood up. Rex said: 'It looks like we've got ourselves a job.'

Pete did not answer. They moved quickly between the tables towards the Ashanti.

He was within a few paces of his own table, when they intercepted him. Rex had his hands bunched in his tunic pockets. Pete was lighting a stub of a cigarette.

Rex said quietly: 'Okay, big boy. Put her down.'

Whether the Ashanti normally understood the complexities of the American idiom was doubtful. But in this case there could be no doubting Rex's meaning.

A sudden silence in the wineshop was broken only by the gasping of the woman as she continued her useless struggle.

The grin faded from the Ashanti's face. And now they were at close quarters Rex could see that it had the traditional cast of a brutalised thug. He was not typical of his race. His type appeared in all races and in all colours. The type that finds its greatest pleasure in inflicting suffering on the weak.

He tried to push past Rex.

Rex was no lightweight, but the Ashanti was much heavier and was the taller by a clear inch. He might have succeeded if Pete had not been there.

Pete had the English habit of doing most things casually — as though nothing was really worth bothering about. There was something very casual, but none the less effective, about the way he slowly placed his heavy boot on one of the Ashanti's thinly sandalled feet. Then, with meticulous detachment, he pressed down with all his weight.

The Ashanti came to an abrupt stop. He grunted with pain.

It was Rex's turn to smile.

'D'you get the idea, bud?' he asked. 'We want you to put the dame down.'

Pete maintained the pressure on his foot. The Ashanti's lips twisted and his eyes showed more white than usual. But he still held on to the woman. There was a faint movement of chairs. The Ashanti's drinking companions, the two Touareg Arabs, had risen and were coming up behind Rex and Pete. Each was fingering the folds of his burnous — fingering for a knife.

Almost immediately there was another and much louder scuffle from all parts of the wineshop. It was created by the dozen or so legionnaires who were at the tables. They advanced on the Touaregs.

It was probable that most of those legionnaires had very little sympathy with a white woman who was stupid enough to get herself into such a situation. But they had no intention of watching two of their comrades knifed in the back — which the Touaregs were fully capable of doing.

The remaining customers were composed mostly of Arabs, with a sprinkling of blacks. They, too, stood up. They watched the legionnaires with a smouldering malevolence. The situation had the makings of a particularly ugly brawl. A brawl in which the legionnaires would be outnumbered by at least three to one.

Rex realised this as he took a swift look round. It was forbidden for legionnaires to carry arms when off duty in Sadazi. It was also forbidden for the civil population. But whereas the legionnaires had to observe the order, it was certain that all the others were armed. All would have knives. Quite a few would have pistols, too.

Somehow the clash had to be averted. The key lay with the Ashanti. The Ashanti had to be overpowered and humiliated before the others had time to react. If that happened, there was just a chance that the storm would pass, for the Arabs, particularly, set great store by personal dignity. They would not willingly commit themselves to the support of a man who had already been made to look a fool.

But speed was the vital factor. Something had to be done within a few seconds.

Rex stepped aside, then took a long, lightning-fast pace. It brought him behind the Ashanti. He had a confused glimpse of the woman's blonde head hanging over a black shoulder. Then he did two things simultaneously. He linked his hands round the Ashanti's forehead and pulled. And he pressed a knee in the Ashanti's spine and pushed,

It was a quick way to kill a man. A way

he had learned when a G.I. It was a technique that had been perfected by British Commandos, then passed on to the American Army during the war . . .

But Rex had no intention of killing the Ashanti. He had to gauge the conflicting pressures so that the man became helpless with pain — but no more. If his back broke he would be dead in a moment.

The Ashanti moaned. Every muscle of his powerful body became bunched, as though paralysed by cramp. He lost his grip on the woman.

She slipped sideways off his shoulder and hit the floor softly. When that happened Rex removed his hands from the Ashanti's forehead. Then he drew back his right hand and hit him a downward chopping blow with the edge of his palm at the spot where the spinal column joined the back of the head. For two silent seconds the Ashanti remained standing. Then he gave a faint and uncontrolled cough, like that of a child. He took a reeling step, knocking over a table before he collapsed forwards over a chair.

Pete took a quick look at him, pulling up his eyelids and feeling his pulse.

Then he said: 'I don't think we need concern ourselves any longer with this amorous gentleman. He'll be all right. But I don't think he'll be feeling quite himself for some time.'

There was a laugh from a few of the legionnaires. That broke the tension. The Arabs — and even some of the blacks — looked with contempt at the prostrate Ashanti. There was a move back to the tables.

The woman had got to her feet. For the first time, Rex was able to get a close look at her It confirmed his first impression. There was more than mere physical beauty in that face of hers.

There was cool strength there, too. It showed in the level set of her blue eyes. In the rich emphasis of her mouth. And it was attested by her demeanour at this moment. Her hair was disarrayed. Dust from the floor was smeared on her cheeks. Her dress was torn at the top. She had just been subjected to almost primeval violence. But there was no suggestion of hysteria about her.

Rex said: 'Are you okay?'

She hesitated, then said in accented English: 'Yes — due to you and your friend.'

'Think nothing of it. I guess you're a stranger to Sadazi?'

'I've just arrived.'

'I guessed so. Well, let me tell you something. Keep out of joints like this unless you've got a big party with you. Arab wineshops ain't any place for you tourist dames.'

She smiled faintly. It was the sort of quick, deep smile that shows a real sense of humour.

'I know that now — I think I'd better get out of here.'

'No, not yet.'

She looked surprised.

'I don't understand. Why not? You've just said it's no place for a woman.'

'And I wasn't kidding any, lady. But you can't leave here alone. After what's happened, you'll know why. We'll take you back to the European quarter — but we'd like time to finish our wine first. So maybe you'll help us drink it?'

She smiled again.

'Of course . . . if you don't think there'll be any more . . . '

'No one else will try to touch you here. You can relax.'

Pete picked her wide-brimmed sun hat from the floor and gave it to her. Curious eyes watched them as they went to the table. But there was no animosity. The passions that had simmered up in a moment had subsided as quickly.

Rex got another glass from an un-savoury-looking Bormone waiter. She hesitated when he filled it. Then she said in her heavy but fascinating foreign accent: 'Will you let me pay . . . ?' And she gestured towards the small leather bag, which hung from her shoulder.

'It's okay,' Rex said. 'There's plenty left in the bottle.'

'Yes But legionnaires are not very rich, uh?'

'That's pitching it soft.' She looked puzzled, so he added: 'We're the world's cheapest army, except maybe for the Russians and the Chinese. But me — I'm okay. I'm a gambler and I've won. So drink and forget it.'

She sipped the red wine. She did not speak. Both Rex and Pete noticed that even when silent she could be completely relaxed — which was rare for a woman, particularly a young woman.

Pete groped in the breast pocket of his *capote*. He pulled out a paper packet. There were three cigarettes in it and one half-consumed stub. She was about to accept the offer when she saw the stub. She flipped open the catch to her shoulder bag and produced a small silver case. It was filled tight with European cigarettes. Cigarettes that they had rarely seen in years.

'Will you try these instead?'

They did. And when they were all smoking Rex decided to put the question that was on his mind. He hitched his chair a little closer to the table. Then he said: 'What gave you the crazy idea to come here on your own?'

She inhaled deeply before answering.

'It was a mistake.'

'It sure was. I guess you're a tourist.

Most of you folks have guides. Weren't you told to keep clear of the native quarter?'

'I'm not a tourist, although I came up from Oran with a party of them. I took the train as far as Baruta, then we had to take camels. I didn't like that.'

That was the usual tourist route to Sadazi. The railhead was at Beruta, and many of them faded out of the trip when told that the last lap was over ninety miles of desert on sullen camels

With his usual Brooklyn bluntness, Rex asked: 'If you're not a tourist, what brought you out here?'

She did not hesitate.

'I came to see my husband, and I'm afraid I was so anxious to find him that I got lost. He's a legionniaire. Perhaps you know him. His name is Tovak. I am Annice Tovak.'

At the far end of the wineshop an Arab girl started to sing a tuneless dirge and waggle her thin, semi-nude body. A drunken legionnaire shouted an obscenity at her. There was a multi-lingual roar of protest.

But Rex, and Pete heard none of it. Their minds, all of their senses, were numb.

It was as though a potent anaesthetic had been injected into the parts of the brain that controlled the power to see, to hear, to smell, to taste, to feel.

But the effect wore off. Gradually, they realised that she was still speaking. And, because she was staring at the tabletop, she had not noticed anything unusual about them.

' . . . it took a long time to arrange an exit permit out of Czechoslovakia,' she was saying. 'But it was done in the end. I went to Paris first, to see if they would discharge my husband from the Legion. They would not. They could not. They said he would have to serve another two years. So there was only one thing for me to do. I had to come here to see him. To tell him I'd be waiting . . . '

She broke off. She raised her eyes and looked at them. Pete made a desperate effort and formulated a question.

'Did — did you expect to find him in one of these places?'

His voice sounded raw and it shook. She seemed mildly surprised by it. And by the taut expression on both their faces. But she answered normally.

'No — I don't think so. I was looking for the Legion barracks. But it was dark and I got lost. But when I saw a wineshop with legionnaires in it I knew one of you would help me — so you see, I don't want to stay here. I want to go to the barracks to find my husband . . . I suppose they will let me see him straight away . . . ?'

There was a sudden note of urgent anxiety in her voice.

She added: 'After so many years . . . I don't want to wait another hour. You understand . . . ?'

She looked at them — questioningly, appealingly.

Rex gazed through the window and into the blackness of the alley beyond. Pete stared fixedly at his fingernails. Anything was better than looking at her.

The skinny little Arab wench wailed and jigged. The drunken legionnaire was being helped out by two of his friends.

Rex thought: 'This can't be happening.

I'm gonna wake up.'

Pete thought: 'One of us has to tell her . . . Oh, God! Why does it have to be one of us . . . ?'

Suddenly Annice leaned forward across the table.

She said: 'What's the matter? Why are you quiet? Isn't he here? They told me in Paris he was stationed at Sadazi. Has he been moved?'

Pete cleared his throat. He continued to look at his fingernails as he answered.

'No,' he said slowly, flatly, 'he is still in Sadazi . . . I — I don't think you'll be allowed to move him. I'm sorry . . . '

'Move him? Please — what do you mean?'

Pete gathered himself. It had to be done.

'He's dead.'

She had been holding her glass. It twisted out of her hand and rolled to the floor, splashing red liquid on her dress. Her under lip twitched.

Suddenly they could hear her breathing deep and fast, like someone in a fever.

'How long?'

35

'Since this morning.'

'What was the illness?'

Here it was! The worst question of all.

Pete said: 'It was not an illness.'

She touched her flaxen hair. An aimless gesture with a shaking hand.

'You mean . . . there was an accident . . . ?'

'He was executed. You see . . . he killed a man while trying to desert. He wanted to reach you.'

It was out! It was told in three wretched sentences. Sentences that summarised the extinction of one life, and would probably wreck another.

She was silent for a long time. And during that time they knew that hot brands of suffering were searing into her soul. Their imprint would be with her for so long as she lived.

Eventually, Pete said: 'We'll take you to the barracks. I'm sure Colonel Jeux will see you.'

'Is he the commanding officer?'

'Yes — a new one. He's only been here a few weeks.'

'Did he have anything to do with the execution?'

'Colonel Jeux was president of the court martial.'

'Then he is a murderer!'

She spoke with a controlled ferocity which compelled Pete and Rex to look straight at her.

'You must try to understand,' Pete said softly. 'Your husband killed a legionnaire. The court martial acted according to military law. There was no choice about it.'

Annice breathed out between her white teeth.

The result was a gentle but vibrant hiss.

'Military law! A hooligan law! A law of the Foreign Legion! A civilised army would have given him a discharge, then he would never have needed to desert.'

Pete knew that this was partly true. In such exceptional circumstances, most European armies would have granted Tovak a discharge on compassionate grounds. There would have been delay, of course. And much investigation. But in the end it would have been granted. But not in the Legion. In the Legion any form of compassion was almost unknown. And a man was only given a premature release if he became physically unfit for further service.

Rex retrieved her glass. He filled it with the last of the wine. It was cloudy, unappetising stuff. He pushed it towards her. She ignored it But she looked from Pete to him.

She said: 'Did he . . . was he brave?'

'He sure was,' Rex said uncomfortably. 'He wasn't scared any.'

'I'm glad. I loved him. I'll always love him. But he was never one of the hard ones of the world. He used to think a lot. And like all people who think, he was very afraid of death.'

She changed as she spoke. The venom had gone. Memories had taken over.

But that did not last. It was Rex who changed it all. The impulsive, well-meaning Rex, whose sense of diplomacy was on par to that of a steam hammer.

He said: 'He was okay when he died — and it was all over before he knew much about it. We didn't waste time once . . . '

Rex faded out as she looked hard at him.

'Were you there? You saw it all . . . ?'

Pete felt sweat ooze out of his forehead and then cold upon it. He tried to retrieve the situation.

'It's as Rex says. We know he showed plenty of courage.'

'You're not answering me. Were you there?'

Pete dropped his cigarette on the floor and stubbed it out with his toe. Then he slackened his *ceinture*, as if finding the twelve-inch waist sash too warm. She watched him. Waiting.

There was no escape.

'Yes,' Pete said. 'We were there.'

'Does the Legion encourage spectators when a man is executed? Is it taken as an entertainment?'

'We were not spectators.'

Her eyes seemed to change both in shade and in form. They became a pale and an utterly hard blue. And flat. Small. As though sinking into the skull.

'You shot him?'

'We were in the firing squad . . . we had no choice about it. None of us liked it. But it was orders and we . . . '

Her open hand slashed across his cheek. The sound was like a shot from a small pistol. The Arab girl ceased singing. Every customer ceased talking. They all stared.

Pete did not move. But a flush of high colour ran under his tan.

She stood up. She scarcely moved her lips as she spoke. Yet each word could be heard in every corner of the place. They came out like chips of ice.

'A few hours ago you helped to kill a good, civilised, cultured man. You did it because you are the willing slaves of a barbaric army. An army that deserves its reputation as a throwback to the dark ages. Men, I tell you — *real* men . . . would not serve in it. They would not tolerate its foul system . . .

'Your Legion . . . it is a resort of the jackboot and the tyrant and the frightened bondsmen. Sometimes, through tragedy, people like my husband find themselves in it. But not for long! Men like he are driven to crime and then executed in the name of military law! The Legion . . . it is blood on the doorstep of

France . . . it is an affront to all humanity and the peoples of North Africa ought to rid themselves of it . . . '

She paused, as if gathering her thoughts in preparation for more. But she changed her mind. She turned abruptly to the door.

Rex and Pete remained seated. They remained very still.

She had spoken in English and with a heavy Slavonic accent. But the gist of her words would certainly be understood by many of the Arabs in the wineshop. And within a few hours news of the outburst, no doubt exaggerated, would spread all through Sadazi and beyond. It could have a bad effect. The Arabs were sharing in the general resurgence of nationalism. An incident such as this, trivial though it might be, could only result in giving fresh confidence to the troublemakers.

The fact that her accusations were grossly inaccurate did not matter. Here was a white woman damning the Legion in a native wineshop. It was unheard of. But it was true. Skilful tongues could make much of it in repetition.

Rex summarised their thoughts.

'She's made us look like a couple of mugs,' he said. 'And I guess she's caused a whole lot of harm, too. But we can't blame her. And we can't sit around while she walks out of here alone. We'll have to see that she's okay.'

'I don't think that will be necessary,' Pete said dryly. 'Look.'

Rex looked.

Annice was standing by the door. She was not alone. A Touareg Arab was talking to her. His robes were somewhat richer than most. He carried himself with an air of assured authority.

She was listening to him. Listening intently. Several times she nodded, as though indicating emphatic agreement. Then she turned back with him into the wineshop.

They went to a remote table in a quiet corner.

They were still sitting there when Rex and Pete had to leave for midnight *appel*.

3

Operational Order

Colonel Jeux wrestled with the document. But he could make little sense of it. It ran to four closely typed pages, comprising eleven sections and fifteen sub-sections. It was headed: *Operational Order For Protection of Oil Pipe Line in Tutana Region*. It was from the High Command, Algiers. And it was addressed to he, Colonel Jeux, commanding officer of the Legion garrison at Dini Sadazi. It was a confidential document. It was a vital document, calling for immediate action. But it defied Jeux's drink-addled brain.

Once, with a great effort, he was able to comprehend the meaning of the entire first page. But as soon as he turned to page two the import of page one was forgotten. And by the time he got half way down page three the whole document had become a mess of fuddled phrases.

43

So he started again. This time, he tried reading it aloud. The result was just as unsatisfactory. Worse, if anything. For the sound of his own voice increased the violence of his headache.

There was only one thing to do. He must have a drink — even though it was early in the morning.

He rose wearily from behind his steel desk, and went to a steel filing cabinet. The bottom drawer was labelled 'Miscellaneous'. He unlocked it and produced a half-full bottle of Bisquit Dubouche and a tumbler. Colonel Jeux looked very old and very sad as he poured himself a long drink.

And as he drank it greedily he thought: 'It is ruining me — but what can I do? I am useless — *oui*, useless — without it.'

He was, he realised, typical of too many senior officers. Long years of boredom in sweltering and unhealthy garrison towns such as this, years in which he had seen none but the same faces and repeated the same routines, had led to a constantly increasing consumption of brandy. At first it had been a solace. It freed him from the dragging chains of reason and let his mind soar to the stars. Under its influence he had thought as the poets think, saw things as the philosophers saw them. Brandy had made life tolerable.

But not now.

Now the stuff had half paralysed his mind. Drink enough of it and he could think — after a fashion. Do without it, and he was a weak, helpless creature.

Ah! The tragedy of it all.

As the liquid warmed and caressed his vitals, Colonel Jeux thought of the Man He Might Have Been.

Thirty years ago he had been the senior cadet of his class at St. Maixent. His marking had been the highest ever known in the history of that military college. 'Jeux,' they had said, 'has a brilliant brain. One day he will be a general . . . '

And he had thought so, too. Particularly when, as a lieutenant, his thesis on the use of cavalry in desert warfare had been adopted as a standard work.

Now look at him! Look at what the years and the brandy had done . . . He was fortunate indeed to have reached his present rank. Thank God the High Command did no more than suspect that his brain was rotting. Rotting in a bath of alcohol.

This document, which lay on his desk . . .

Any pimply-faced sous lieutenant would be able to understand it. But not he. Not Jeux.

He poured more brandy into the tumbler and went back to his desk. He started to read again, sipping frequently. It was a little better this time.

The main points became fairly clear and he was able to retain them in his mind. But it was too much of an effort to follow the details.

It seemed that oil from the new refineries at Reggan was to be pumped across a thousand miles of desert to the naval base at Oran. There it would refuel the fleets of the Western powers.

The pipes were almost completed and pumping was due to start within a fortnight.

But — and this was the important point — there had been several recent instances of damage to the pipes in the Tutana region. The High Command was of the opinion that this must be the result of action by the Touareg tribes. There were two reasons for this opinion. Firstly, the *Bureau Arabe* — a security department dealing with Arab affairs — had reported sudden activity by the Touaregs in the area. Secondly, the Touaregs were known to be hostile to the oil plan, claiming that the pipes infringed their territorial rights.

It was therefore required that he, Colonel Jeux, make dispositions for the protection of the oil supply. And he was also to take any necessary action to subdue the Touaregs.

That was the bare essence of the eleven sections and the fifteen sub-sections.

The remainder of the operational order was concerned with the number of troops to be employed, arrangements for replacements at Sadazi, lines of liaison with the Bureau, channels of reports to the High Command . . .

Jeux blinked uncomprehendingly at them.

He rubbed his thin, wrinkled face. He had no choice about it. He would have to call for assistance. He would have to get someone to explain it all, then take over the administrative work from him.

Strictly speaking, the man for such a task was the staff adjutant, Major Baya. But Jeux dismissed such a notion as soon as he thought of it.

No doubt, Major Baya would explain it all very competently. But while doing so, there would be a cynical note in his voice and a light of ugly amusement in his eye. Baya would also do all the necessary organising with smooth efficiency. But at the same time he would be secretly sneering at his commanding officer. Talking in the mess. Saying that Jeux was a drunken fool. That Jeux ought to be relieved of his command.

Jeux knew that his adjutant said these things. They frightened him. Why? Because they were true.

Non, Baya must not know that he, Jeux, was incapable of following a command order.

Monclaire was the man.

Captain Monclaire was very senior and very experienced in his rank. He had an exceptional record of active service. And he was a man to be trusted. People instinctively trusted Monclaire.

Oui, Monclaire would help. And he would not patronise. He would not talk.

For Jeux knew that Monclaire understood him. Understood why the barren years had destroyed a once brilliant and finely poised mind. And, because of his understanding, he sympathised.

It must be Monclaire.

Jeux touched the bell on his desk. He gave an order to the orderly corporal.

Then he picked up the bottle of brandy. He corked it and carefully relocked it in the drawer labelled 'Miscellaneous'.

But he forgot about the tumbler. He left that — still with a little liquid in it — standing conspicuously on his desk.

★ ★ ★

Monclaire did not give a direct explanation of the command order. He discussed

49

the document with Jeux, and during the discussion he made each detail clear. It was typical of Monclaire's tact and Jeux was grateful for it.

Monclaire made the numerical deployments understandable when, after glancing at the typed sheets, he said: 'Since you are forbidden to detach more than one quarter of your garrison strength, I take it that you have decided to send a single complete company to the Tutana area?'

Jeux nodded eagerly.

'*Oui*, it is so. I had decided to send a company.'

'My company is available, *mon colonel*.'

'Ah.'

Jeux hesitated. The hint was clear enough. But he did not want Monclaire to disappear into the desert for several weeks. In his short time as commander at Sadazi, Jeux had come to rely on this smallish, gaunt-faced captain. But on the other hand, Monclaire wanted to go. That was obvious. And his experience in desert operations was probably unequalled. He would make no mistake about protecting the oil line.

So Jeux said reluctantly: 'It will be your company, *capitaine*.'

'*Bon* . . . Since section nine gives the operational codes, perhaps I had better take a copy now.'

'*Oui*, by all means.'

'And since my company must be equipped with radio, I will arrange for twenty-four hour call signs.'

'Quite so — quite so.'

'These map references — I'll have them confirmed with Algiers immediately. That is what you wish, is it not?'

'Ah, certainly . . . '

Point by point Monclaire interpreted the document and took over responsibility for it. Finally, it was arranged that his company should leave for the Tutana region at dawn on the following day. They would be based near the village of Tutana itself, which they would reach in four days' marching time.

Then Monclaire put down the document. He said slowly: 'There is one other matter, *mon colonel*. Two of my legionnaires requested an interview with me this morning. It was granted, of course.

51

They reported an extraordinary series of incidents in a wineshop last night which bear closely on the execution of Legionnaire Tovak.'

Jeux looked up slowly.

'Tovak! A nasty business that. I didn't like it, *capitaine*!'

'So was the sequel . . . '

Monclaire repeated the events of the previous evening. Several times, in response to interruptions by Jeux, he had to repeat himself. The colonel had some difficulty in understanding the precise sequence of events. He probably would never have understood them had it not been for Monclaire's patience and lucidity.

When, at last, the story was completed and comprehended, Jeux said diffidently: 'These two legionnaires — might they have exaggerated?'

'I don't think so. One is English, the other American. While on a recent operation, I discovered that the Englishman once held a commission in the British army. He has a certain cynical indifference to most things, but he's an excellent soldier and reliable. The American served during the World War in his own army. Like so many others, he joined the Legion out of boredom. He, too, is a good soldier. And he is trustworthy. I accept their story without hesitation.'

'Ah . . . '

Colonel Jeux made a feeble gesture with his left hand. It fluttered towards the filing cabinet.

'This calls for careful consideration, *capitaine*. I do not usually drink at this hour, but perhaps a . . . '

Monclaire smiled and nodded. He did not want brandy. But he made it easier for his commanding officer by indicating that he did.

Jeux reproduced the bottle. He fumbled anxiously in the drawer for the tumbler.

'*Dieu* . . . I could swear there were two glasses in here. I put one of them back when I last had a drink yesterday . . . but one of them seems to be missing . . . '

Monclaire said quietly: 'Let me see, *mon colonel*.'

Unobserved, he picked the missing tumbler from the desk, emptied the few remaining drops of liquid on the floor.

Then, concealing it behind his hand, he pushed it to the back of the drawer. He fumbled for a moment and drew it out again.

'It was there, *mon colonel*. It had rolled to the far comer.'

'*Bon*.'

They drank. Monclaire slowly. Jeux quickly. When he had finished, Jeux seemed a little more sure of himself. His sentences were formulated with less hesitation.

He said: 'Perhaps I ought to see this woman.'

'I think so. Apart from any damage she may do, we are responsible for her safety while she is in this area. It is rather ominous that immediately after creating a scene in the wineshop she was seen in close conversation with a Touareg. It suggests that the Touaregs may try to make use of her.'

'Make use of her! In what way?'

'You will remember that during the court martial it was revealed that during the World War she was an active resistance worker. She was something of an expert in sabotage and explosives.'

Jeux put down his glass. He stared at Monclaire.

'You really believe . . . ah, *non* . . . '

'I don't believe anything like that at the moment, *mon colonel*. But we must keep in mind that a woman such as she *could* be of great value to the Touaregs now they are suspected of sabotaging the oil line.'

'*Oui* . . . it is so. I'll have her sent back to Oran immediately.'

'But, no doubt, you'll wish to see her first — as you suggested. It would be better if you could persuade her that it is in her own interest to leave. And perhaps you can convince her that the death of her husband does not make us murderers.'

Jeux nodded dimly.

'Send for her. Bring her to me — and — and perhaps you would care to be at the interview, *capitaine*.'

* * *

Monclaire went to the *Hotel Afrique* — a grandiloquent title for Sadazi's shabby and only tourist accommodation.

The black desk clerk gave an insolent shrug.

'Madame Tovak? Yes, she reserved a room.'

'Where is she?'

'She did not come.'

'Did she let you know?'

The man shook his head. Despite the dry heat, he was clad in a formal black western suit with a starched collar. Sweat oozed down his face. But he was obviously too proud of the garments to consider replacing them with something more appropriate.

Monclaire put his last question.

'How did she make the reservation?'

'By telegraph from Oran.'

Monclaire sucked the knob of his cane. Inwardly, he cursed the woman. This was exasperating. She would have to be found. And the main task of finding her would be his.

He returned briskly to the barracks. The next move was obvious. A patrol would have to search the native quarter. If necessary, it would have to go through each house, each bistro, each café even each squalid brothel . . .

The English and the American legionnaires would have to be in the patrol for identification purposes, for only they had seen the Tovak woman closely and clearly.

Monclaire gave the orders with his usual crisp decision. But he was worried. Very worried. And for good reason. It was not only concern for the woman. It was also a matter of the sort of reception a search patrol would receive in the native quarter.

They were always resented — naturally. And for that reason such patrols had scarcely ever been seen in recent years. The sudden arrival of one now — when the atmosphere was already strained — might result in an ugly incident.

But there was no choice about it. If there was going to be trouble, then trouble had to be faced

4

Search Patrol

At midday a section of twenty men under Captain Monclaire left the barracks and marched towards the native quarter.

They were in light battle order — rifle, bayonet in scabbard, plus leather ammunition pouches. That was all. Deliberately Monclaire had cut their equipment. He wished to avoid a clash if he could, and he knew that nothing was more likely to inflame the Arabs than the sight of Legionnaires dressed as though for a campaign. A touch of informality was needed.

As they approached the narrow streets Monclaire gave an order.

'*Repos!*'

Lebel straps were slackened and the rifles slung over their shoulders. The patrol marched at ease, talking.

Rex was in the front file with Pete. He

said: 'It's going to be one helluva job trying to find her — if she's still here.'

Pete glanced at him.

'You think she could be dead?'

'Yep, murdered, and the body put away in some nice quiet place. I don't like to think of that happening, but it wouldn't surprise me any!'

'It would surprise me,' Pete said firmly. 'I've an idea the Touaregs could find a better use for Annice than assaulting and murdering her. She could have a big propaganda value.'

Rex did not answer. He was thinking about her. About her flaxen hair, the slimness of her body, the delicate strength of her face. She was, he decided, the sort of woman who stayed in a guy's mind . . .

Like many Americans, Rex was an immature romantic where women were concerned. He assumed a façade of tough indifference towards them, but it was not a convincing one.

The patrol passed the edge of the cobbled market square and entered Rue St. Jean.

Rue St. Jean was unique in Sadazi.

At one time its twenty spacious western houses had been occupied by French traders. But gradually the prosperous Arabs had moved into them and the French had moved out — taking refuge in the *Hotel Afrique*. Now the comparatively wide street — modelled on a typical French *chemin* — was entirely the domain of the East. It was an example of colonisation in reverse. And it was here that the search was to begin.

As they entered the street, a large and rapidly increasing crowd of Arabs were following the patrol. They were the usual hotch-potch. Arrogant young men and shuffling, diseased old beggars. Yattering children and sloe-eyed women.

All curious. All ready to be hostile.

Monclaire halted the patrol. He detached four legionnaires. Two were posted at either end of the street with orders to allow no one in or out.

The others were divided into a couple of parties, one under Monclaire and the other commanded by Sergeant Zatov, a giant-sized Ukranian.

Pete was with Monclaire's party, which

took the north side. Rex went with Zatov.

Zatov had received detailed orders before he left the barracks. He repeated them.

'We have,' he said in a voice which seemed to rumble out of the depth of his belly, 'to be careful — careful!'

He repeated the word on an inflexion of astonished contempt. Then, with a darting movement of his left hand, he picked a fly out of his red beard. Thus relieved, he continued: 'We are to look for a woman . . . If any legionnaire smiles, I, Zatov, will squeeze out his eyeballs! What sort of woman you ask? I will tell you. She is white. She is missing. And Legionnaire Tyle knows her — but that's not why we want to find her . . . '

Sergeant Zatov twisted up the corners of his mouth. The legionnaires recognised the signal and obeyed it. It meant that they had permission to show appreciation of his humour. All of them laughed briefly. All except Rex. Not that Rex resented the feeble quip. He was thinking about Annice Tovak. And wondering why a nagging worry about her was biting into the recesses of his mind.

The search of the first house was completed within five minutes. The owner — who made a lush living by importing trinket souvenirs for tourists — protested only mildly.

It was much the same in the second house.

The crisis came in the third Arab home.

This was rather larger than most of the others, and it was well known as the property of Tu el Adaa, who owned several of Sadazi's many wineshops.

The building was surrounded by a small cactus garden. At one time the garden had been well kept. But now, since Adaa had little interest in horticulture, it was little more than a mass of struggling and disillusioned foliage.

A Bormone servant opened the double teak door. Zatov waved a typewritten document in front of him.

'I've the commandant's warrant to search this place,' he announced, and pushed his way in. The others followed, their boots ringing harshly on the tesselated hall flooring.

Here Zatov turned again to the servant. 'I want to see Adaa.'

Before the servant could answer, Adaa appeared.

He was a Touareg. But unlike most Touaregs, there was little of the warrior about his appearance. He was short and he was grossly fat. His robes swathed him like a cloth round a bulging cheese. His face was a circle of brown flesh into which all the features had submerged. All except his eyes. His eyes stood out because of their level intensity. They never moved, they never blinked. They were like the eyes of a dead man.

Adaa rolled rather than walked into the hall from one of the rooms.

'You want to speak with me?'

His voice had a high, almost feminine pitch, which emerged strangely from his obese body.

'I am going to search your house,' Zatov said curtly.

Adaa did not appear perturbed.

'Why?'

Zatov told him. The reaction was unexpected. Adaa made a faintly insolent gesture with his hands.

'There is no need for a search. The lady is here.'

There was a moment of complete silence while Zatov absorbed the words. During that time his bearded chin hung loose and he stared blankly at the Touareg.

He repeated stupidly: 'The lady is here . . . '

'Certainly.' Adaa spoke his French smoothly, confidently.

'Then bring her to me. I have orders to take her to the commanding officer. And I'll . . . '

The words faded out. A woman, young and blonde, stood in the doorway from which Adaa had emerged. She stood with a hand on a slender, shapely hip. She was watching them with a cold, almost icy detachment.

Rex took in a sharp breath. And he felt a rush of relief. No harm had come to her . . .

Zatov stared — as they all stared at her. Almost reluctantly, he eventually turned to Rex.

'Is that her, legionnaire?'

At first Rex did not hear the words. It was when they were repeated in a thunder-like bawl that he nodded.

Zatov jerked a thumb at one of the legionnaires.

'Tell the *capitaine*.'

There was an interval of no more than a couple of minutes before Monclaire arrived. But it was a period of mounting curiosity for Rex, and of shuffling uncertainty for the others. Annice Tovak remained motionless and silent, framed like a picture by the arch of the doorway. Adaa stood equally still in the centre of the hall. But there was a suggestion of relaxed confidence about him. He did not look like a man who was going to have a lot of explaining to do.

Monclaire looked as if a great load of anxiety had suddenly been lifted from his shoulders as he strode into the hall.

Zatov called his men to attention and saluted.

'This,' he said, indicating Annice, 'is the woman. Legionnaire Tyle has identified her, *mon capitaine*.'

Monclaire moved towards her and saluted. She stared through him. She did not acknowledge the salute by even the smallest movement.

'Madame Tovak?'

Slowly, very slowly, she parted her lips. Her voice was quiet, but strong.

'I am Madame Tovak — a widow.'

Mondaire hesitated. Then he said softly: 'I am sorry, madame. We are all sorry. And I am under orders to escort you to my commanding officer so that he may explain . . . '

'Will explanations bring my husband back?'

'It would be better if you understood all that happened.'

'I know all that happened. And I know that you are an officer of the army that murdered him. An army of barbarians, monsieur. So please tell your commanding officer that I shall not see him and neither shall I have anything to do with any other member of the Legion.'

The words came louder and faster. They were impelled by emotion. The emotion of unadulterated hate.

Monclaire stroked his small moustache. The hand that did so shook with anger, which he controlled with difficulty.

'You are making a mistake, *madame*. I repeat — I must ask you to come with us. It is, in any case, most undesirable for you to be in this place. I will not ask how you came to arrive here, but you must leave it.'

'And if I refuse?'

'If you refuse, we shall be compelled to take you by force.'

She moved her mouth in a grim caricature of a smile.

'So it seems that the Legion also abducts women!'

'*Madame*! I — '

'You are very brave, *monsieur capitaine*! You and all the other legionnaires. It must need great courage for you to risk using force against one woman. I congratulate you!'

A pulse started to twitch at the side of Monclaire's neck. He was aware of a mass of seething uncertainties. Only a few minutes previously, he had doubted whether the woman would be found at all. And if she was found, he had expected her to be grateful for the fact. This situation was beyond any of his calculations.

'For the last time, *madame* . . . '

Adaa interrupted. Adaa had been watching and listening while retaining his aura of composed confidence. Now he walked heavily up to Monclaire and piped: 'I do not think the *capitaine* has any power to take the lady away against her will. She has not committed any offence, so she must be allowed her freedom.'

Monclaire turned and faced Adaa. He stared back into the blank, dead eyes.

'You had better be quiet, Adaa. Already you are in enough trouble. The *Bureau Arabe* may wish to question you about this.'

Annice raised her thin eyebrows. She said: 'It is no use trying to bully us. Adaa has done nothing, either, except give me shelter. You cannot remove me from his home, or punish him for offering me hospitality.'

'While you are in this area, *madame*,

your safety is the concern of the Legion, acting on behalf of the government of France. We are empowered to take any necessary measures for your protection.'

'But I am in no danger. There has been no threat of danger. If you touch me *capitaine*, the result could be very serious. Remember I am a foreign national holding a passport. The matter would be taken up with the French Colonial Department.'

Monclaire breathed heavily. He had to acknowledge the truth of her words. There was no fragment of evidence that would justify her removal from the Arab's house . . . unless . . .

He glanced towards Rex.

'Legionnaire Tyle.'

Rex clicked to attention.

'Capitaine.'

'Did Annice Tovak make threats against France and the Legion when you saw her in the wineshop?'

Rex looked at her before replying. She was watching him. And there was now a new expression on her face. An expression that Rex had not seen before. It was one which seemed to blend contempt with sympathy. Just as free humanity might look upon a willing slave. In that second he almost hated her.

'She said that the Legion was blood on the doorstep of France, *mon capitaine.* And that North Africans ought to rid themselves of the Legion . . . '

It was Monclaire's turn to offer a humourless smile.

He said to her: 'You understand, *madame.* You have been inciting disaffection among French subjects. I will have to hold you for an inquiry.'

Her hands dropped slowly from her hip. Her body became taut.

But her reaction was unexpected.

She seemed to surrender. As though accepting the inevitable, she walked towards the door. It was a stately walk. Monclaire was a pace behind her, with the legionnaires following.

It was when they emerged into Rue St. Jean that they glimpsed the gathering storm.

A mumbling roar came from both ends of the street. It surged and faded like wind in the sand. It rose from the Arab crowds — and it was caused by the sight of Annice. Her outburst in the wineshop had had the expected effect. Already she held the status of a martyr in the native quarter.

And she exploited the situation. She raised her hands very slightly, in a gesture of helpless supplication. Then she smiled. It was a gentle, heroic smile, and it was turned full on the Arabs.

Watching her, Rex mumbled: 'The bitch — the beautiful bitch! She's gonna make more trouble . . . '

It certainly seemed so. For a new roar of sympathy and indignation burst from the crowds. This time it was louder. It lasted longer.

Then there was a sudden surge forward. At each end of the street, the crowds — now becoming a mob — forced back the sentries, who would otherwise have been engulfed. But after the first rush, the advance became more cautious. The Arabs were not yet fully inflamed and none wanted to be the first to risk a Lebel bullet.

Monclaire gave a hand signal. The

complete section — except for the four legionnaires who were struggling helplessly with the Arabs — formed a double file.

Pete again found himself next to Rex. And Pete said dryly: 'Perhaps it would have been better if you hadn't found the woman. This is like being crushed in a vice.'

It was precisely what it did look like. From each side the Arabs were advancing like a solid wall.

Rex said: 'It'll be okay. The captain'll handle this.'

But at that moment, Monclaire was experiencing all the loneliness of command. Others need not worry about decisions. He was there to take them. Others could express their fears. He could not. He must always appear calm and confident. He had no one to turn to for support. Yet, his entire career could be in the balance. It was a serious matter for an officer to get himself mixed up in large-scale civil disturbances. If he were to extricate himself without too much trouble, then that would be accepted as his duty. If he made the slightest error, then there would be an enquiry, and he might be dismissed from the Legion.

Monclaire was aware of this as he appraised the position. But the conscious part of his brain was lifting the possibilities from the impossibilities.

Impossible to march away with the woman immediately. Surrounded by the mob, the legionnaires would be completely unable to defend themselves or guard their prisoner.

Possible to hold the mob off until large contingents from the barracks came to clear the streets. In the barracks, they must already be aware that trouble was threatening, for the noise created by the Arabs would be quite audible.

The first move, therefore, was to re-deploy.

He shouted an order. One file marched forward until within ten yards of the Arabs. Then it wheeled to the right and spread out in open order across the road.

A second order, and the remaining file turned about and completed the same manoeuvre at the other end of Rue St. Jean.

The four sweating and grateful sentries

were detached and fell in with their respective files.

The new deployment meant that the legionnaires were standing back to back with about twenty yards between them, and each file was facing the Arabs.

Monclaire turned his attention to Annice. She was standing in the roadway, calm, disinterested. His voice grated as he said: 'I hope you are satisfied with your work, *madame*. But I am afraid you will not be able to see much more. I am going to take you back into Adaa's house and lock you in a room.'

The Arabs sensed that a new conflict was taking place between the Legion officer and the white woman. They ceased to press forward. The medley of their tongues became momentarily still. And as a result, her voice was produced with startling clarity.

'You have made a mistake. I was prepared to come with you to the barracks, since I had no choice. But I am not prepared to be locked up like a common prisoner. There is a limit to what I can accept.'

'It is for your own safety.'

'Safety! It is not me that the Arabs are threatening, *monsieur capitaine*!'

Once again Monclaire found himself breathing hard.

He put a hand on her elbow, intending gently but firmly to guide her inside. She shook herself free. Her slim body was visibly trembling and tortured by fury.

'Don't touch me — murdering swine . . . '

Monclaire decided he had had enough. Hitherto, he had tried to ignore her wild insults, attributing them to a highly emotional state of grief. He was no longer prepared to make any such allowance.

He beckoned to Sergeant Zatov.

'Take her into the house,' he said. 'Tie her hands and lock all doors.'

Zatov rubbed his beard. With the sun on it, it looked as if it was on fire. Looking at Monclaure, Zatov asked slowly: 'Have I permission to use force, *capitaine*?'

Monclaire nodded. There was no time to waste on further attempts at persuasion. A swift glance showed him that the Arabs had paused. That was because they were watching what happened to the woman. When that was settled, they would press forward again. And against them the two lines of legionnaires looked pitifully, almost ridiculously, thin. If the legionnaires were not to be submerged by the mob, they would have to seize the initiative. They would have to act quickly, so as to frighten the Arabs.

Zatov extended a huge hand. It came down on Annice's left shoulder. He gave an effortless flick of his wrist, and she was propelled round on her heels, facing the house. The two operations were completed within a second. She had no opportunity to react. Not until Zatov tried to push her forward.

Then she kicked backwards. Her shoe dug into the tender fibre just below Zatov's knee. He grunted with pain. An ugly shadow came into his eyes.

Like most big men, Sergeant Zatov had a deceptive temperament. In the normal way he appeared to be essentially good-natured, even though he was given to blustering. But the blustering was an integral part of his function as an N.C.O. It was when he was crossed that the basic

Zatov emerged — a man given to uncontrollable rages, which he afterwards regretted. It was one of those rages which had caused him to kill a man when, long ago, he was a lieutenant in the Russian army. After deserting, he had been fortunate to reach west Europe. More fortunate still, to get into the Legion. For here his of violence did not matter so much, and his experience as an officer had led him quickly to the Corporals' School at Saida, in Algeria. Within a few months of being promoted corporal, he had received the third red *galon* of sergeant.

Although Zatov did not know it, there had been several occasions when his name had been considered for a Legion commission. Always it had been regretfully dismissed, his file marked 'Temperamentally unstable.'

It was this instability, this wildness under provocation, which led to disaster now.

As the pain seared up his leg, Zatov felt the familiar clicking in his brain. As though the flimsy bolts of self-control were being picked away. He heard the rush of blood, as he had heard it so often before. And he became conscious of only two facts. A woman was making him seem ridiculous. The woman must suffer.

Zatov was surprisingly agile for a man of such bulk, and he demonstrated the fact now. As Annice twisted to face him, he sprang forward. The back of his right hand flicked across her face. The blow caught her slightly to one side of her forehead — and as she was already turning, the effect was to make her spin completely round before sprawling, face down, on the ground.

He stood over her, his barrel-like chest rising and falling.

But — and this was typical of Zatov — his fury had vanished. It vanished the moment that he struck her. Now he knew shame and regret. Zatov had less compunction about striking a woman than most other Europeans. He could not accept them as being on the same mental or social level as men. Yet, as he looked down on her prostrate form, he realised that his wild temper had created a situation that could be most serious both for him and the entire section.

The probability was emphasised by Monclaire. His voice cut through the fetid air.

'Sergeant Zatov! Stand away from that woman! There may be . . . '

His words were drowned by the Arabs.

The Arabs had been completely silent during Zatov's attack, and for a few seconds after. Now a fresh and still more menacing roar rose from their disordered ranks. It was a roar of completely genuine rage. The white woman, they all knew, was an enemy of the Legion and a champion of their cause. Now, before their indignant eyes, she had been brutally assaulted.

On either side the Arabs were within five or six yards of the Legion files, and were again threatening to surge forward.

Monclaire switched his attention from Zatov to the immediate danger.

Because of the comparatively great width of the street, it had been necessary for the legionnaires to space out so that there was a gap of several feet between each man. The Arabs looked like infiltrating between them. Monclaire knew that if that happened the result would certainly be slaughter. Each legionnaire would be isolated and surrounded. And, realising there was little chance of being detected, plenty of the mob would be willing to push a knife into their ribs.

Monclaire waited for the tumult to die down. He counted on the fact that there was usually a brief spell of pregnant silence before any rabble made a decisive rush. That would be the vital psychological moment when counter measures would be most effective.

The silence came.

It was broken by Monclaire's command.

'*Baionetes!*'

The legionnaires groped for their scabbards. There was an ugly hissing sound as each man drew twenty inches of dull carbonised steel out of a leather covering. There was a short series of clicks as the bayonets were clipped under the Lebel barrels.

'*Fusil!*'

The Lebels were raised to a firing position, each man cuddling the butt of his rifle into his shoulder. And at the same time there was a noise like a faint and hesitant knocking as the safety catches were pressed forward to the free position.

Then Monclaire's voice was heard again — this time in Arabic. He spoke the awkward tongue in slow, simple phrases. But his tones had the penetrating ring of the parade ground.

'If any Arab takes so much as another step forward, the legionnaires will open fire,' he called. 'Your safety is in your own hands. Leave this area immediately.'

It was both a warning to the mob and an order to the legionnaires.

And at first it seemed as though it would at least stabilise the situation until help came from the barracks, for there was an uneasy shuffling among the Arabs.

Until those in the least danger decided to be brave. Until those well removed from the front decided to make a forward rush, pushing the others towards the Lebels.

It was a typical example of those at the back saying 'Forward' and those at the front saying 'Back.'

And, because of weight of numbers, the Arabs at the back had the deciding influence.

At both ends of the street there was a convulsion of robes. The packed humanity seemed to sway without purpose. Then they burst forward.

The volley from the Lebels was mingled with another and more awful sound. The sound of terror and agony. At such extraordinarily short range, the hot slugs caused huge and ghastly wounds. Those who were killed outright were fortunate, for the other casualties fell only to be crushed by countless feet.

Rex felt his rifle nudge his shoulder, and at the same moment he saw a bearded Bormone clutch at his robed belly while blood and fragments of his organs spilled between his fingers.

Pete saw an Arab girl feel for a jawbone that was no longer there, and he thought: 'God . . . I did it . . . I did it.' The knowledge that he could not be blamed, that there was no time to take selective aim, was no consolation.

That single volley was the only one the legionnaires fired.

Before the bolts could be whipped back, before new rounds could be thrust into barrels, the mob was upon them.

5

Rebellion

It was like a hungry sea submerging a few tiny islands.

Each legionnaire was swept with the mob. Each, in fact, became an unwilling part of the mob.

At first, there was no direct attack on them. The Arabs, dazed, frightened and pressed by those at their backs, merely flooded into the centre of Rue St. Jean from both ends.

Rex, after almost falling under the first onslaught, realised that his only chance lay in allowing himself to be carried about by the seething mass of humanity. Most of the others realised that, too.

The shifting pressures against his body were enormous. At one moment Rex thought that an arm was going to be broken. At the next, that a rib would crack inwards. He was dimly aware of a hell of voices in his ears, of a stink of unwashed bodies in his nostrils. Several times he had to fight against a desire to panic — to struggle against the massed movements.

Then, quite suddenly, the pressure eased. The Arabs, having filled the street, had stopped and were looking stupidly around them.

Rex knew that this was only a very temporary respite. In a few moments they would collect their wits. They would remember the carnage. And they would seek vengeance upon those few legionnaires who were sprinkled in their midst . . .

Because he was well above average height, Rex could see over the turbaned heads.

He caught a glimpse of Monclaire. He was pressed against the low wall outside Adaa's house. He seemed to be struggling with someone. Then he saw Pete. Pete was edging towards Monclaire, a look of desperate intensity on his face.

It was the sight of the Englishman that decided Rex. If they were going to be torn to bits, they might as well share their last few moments together.

He pushed in Pete's direction. The distance between them was less than a dozen yards He covered half of it without difficulty. Then the mob around him came to violent life.

It began with a crackling scream that emerged from the throat of an ancient and diseased Touareg woman. The wrinkled hag — whose present misfortunes were entirely her own fault — raised aloft a filthy hand from which a finger had been shot away. Brandishing the blooded stump, she waved in the general direction of Rex.

Other Arabs followed her line of vision. Rex heard a sullen, ugly series of curses. He sensed, rather than saw, that several Arabs were feeling for their knives.

He remembered that he was still holding his rifle. By some chance, it had not been torn from his grasp.

But the first feeling of relief was almost immediately cancelled by the realisation that under such circumstances any rifle would be of little value — and a Lebel of no value at all. For, as every legionnaire knew, the Lebel had many drawbacks as well as advantages. On the credit side, it was accurate, and did not have too much recoil. But on the other hand, it was long and cumbersome. And it took three times as long to load as the British Lee Enfield or the German Mauser. In short, it performed exactly as one would expect of a rifle designed in 1886, and slightly improved in 1893.

And so far as Rex was concerned, at that moment it was as useful as a bow and arrow.

He needed a weapon which would enable him to strike fast and hard at close quarters. The bayonet was the answer.

In a single swift movement he slung the Lebel onto his shoulder and detached the bayonet from the barrel.

He was only Just in time.

The Arab who advanced on him was obviously an expert with the knife. He held the short blade low, at waist level, in preparation for the correct upward cutting movement. And it seemed that his reputation was well established, for the others in the immediate vicinity were content to watch while he attempted the killing.

He was not a big man, that Arab. He was slim, almost slender. But he moved with cat-like grace and speed.

Immediately, Rex knew that if he allowed the Arab to use his speed and skill he would be ripped open within seconds. So he took the only possible course. Instead of waiting for the Arab to get within striking distance, Rex rushed at him.

Rex had a momentary impression of a lean face, of bared teeth, of fluttering robes. Then he thrust forward with the bayonet.

It met no resistance. It pierced only the air.

And the Arab was now standing still — casually, insolently. He had swayed his body only an inch. But it was enough. And he did not bother to make an immediate counter-thrust. Obviously, he intended to enjoy himself with this legionnaire. He intended to demonstrate his mastery before killing at leaisure.

Meantime, by some instinct, the mob

had formed a rough circle round them. What had started as a localised incident was attracting general interest. The spectacle of a bayonet versus knife duel between an Arab and a legionnaire was not a thing that any Arab there would want to miss.

In a dim, disconnected way, Rex realised this. He realised, too, that the duel was detracting attention from the other legionnaires. If he could keep going long enough, the rest of the section might survive . . .

Rex jerked at the Lebel sling and let the rifle slip from his shoulder to the ground. It had been a serious encumbrance. He felt a lot better without it.

The Arab had not moved since Rex's first, futile attack. He was obviously awaiting another — and confident of the outcome.

Rex advanced more slowly this time, but fear was not the reason. He knew that even if, by some miracle, his opponent did not kill him, the mob would surely do so. But he wanted to keep the duel going, to keep the mob's interest centred upon it. If he were to die now, the others would have no chance. If he could delay his death for perhaps a few minutes, then help might arrive from the barracks . . .

Rex gauged the distance. He knew that his extra height, plus the superior length of the bayonet, gave him more than a foot advantage in reach. And that, it seemed, was his only asset.

He tried to make use of it. He made his next thrust when the Arab was barely within distance. The result was ludicrously ineffective. The blade, aimed at the brown throat, passed harmlessly over the robed shoulder.

The Arab smiled. And a guffaw of sadistic amusement rose from the mob. For them, this was indeed rich entertainment. A scene that would bear telling and retelling to those unfortunate enough to miss it.

Then the Arab made his attack.

He began it by moving like a skilled boxer — gliding sideways as well as forward, so that his position was difficult to judge. He made a swift, narrowing circle round Rex, and Rex had to swivel to keep him within vision.

His nine-inch knife was of slender Toledo steel. It seemed to emerge from the folds of his burnous and make a slivering upward streak towards the lower part of Rex's stomach.

Rex tried to jump back. But as he flexed his leg muscles he knew he would be too late. He knew, in an oddly disinterested way, that the blade would enter his vitals within an infinitesimal fraction of a second.

Instead, it penetrated the left sleeve of his tunic. He felt it sliding down the outside of his forearm, shaving away the hair. And he saw the Arab stumble and stagger.

It was his rifle that had saved him. His discarded Lebel. The Arab had put a sandalled foot on it and lost balance at the vital moment.

It was a purely reflex action, which caused Rex to throw down the bayonet and grab the Arab's knife wrist. It was not an act that was in any sense considered or analysed — even momentarily. Yet, like most instinctive actions, it was the correct

91

one. The Arab's transitory mishap had given Rex the opportunity to use the weapon with which he was familiar — his bare hands.

The blade emerged from beneath his ripped sleeve as he started to roll the Arab's wrist in an outward direction. Normally, the result would have been instantaneous. The knife would have fallen from an agonised hand. But these circumstances were far from normal. Both Rex's hand and the Arab's wrist were covered with greasy sweat. It made a firm grip impossible. Before full pressure could be exerted, the Arab pulled and broke free.

And in the same second he made another plunge with the knife.

Rex felt a sharp concentration of pressure over the pit of his stomach. He heard something, too. A harsh, cracking sound.

He saw the weapon. It seemed to be sticking horizontally out of his body. But he was aware of no pain. And fantastically, the knife suddenly fell to the ground.

He realised what had happened. His belt buckle had served as a shield. The blade had been driven against the metal and slipped slightly so that only the extreme point had penetrated a little of the thick black leather. The abruptly arrested impetus had torn it out of the Arab's grasp.

The odds were now even, for neither of them was armed.

Rex switched his attack. He lunged out for the Arab's throat. He got one hand round it, but the Arab twisted away before the tendons could flex.

They watched each other, both breathing heavily. On the Arab's brown face there was now an expression of desperate intensity. He did not like being forced to duel without a weapon. But he was no coward. And he blended agility with cunning.

This was shown when he half turned, as though to retreat into the midst of the mob. Rex made a rush at him. It was another mistake, for the Arab wheeled round and kicked upwards with his sandalled feet. The kick was directed at the base of the belly. Rex managed to twist slightly, and the impact was taken on his thigh. There was a brief flash of pain, which was forgotten when he saw that the Arab had fallen on his back — knocked there by the force of his own kick.

A clear two yards now separated them, but Rex covered the distance with a single downward leap. The Arab tried to squirm away, but Rex landed knees first on his chest. He smelled the man's fetid breath, felt his body tremble under the anticipation of death. But the Arab made one last effort. His fingers, each as straight as an arrow, darted for Rex's eyes. Rex jerked his head aside and felt long, sharp nails scratch his cheeks. Nails that would have gouged out his eyeballs.

The end came with a strange abruptness. Rex knew in a vague way that he had at last got a secure grip on that brown throat. He knew that both his thumbs were pressing on the windpipe. He knew that the whimpering sounds had ceased. But he was surprised to realise that he was attempting to strangle an already dead man. A man whose jaw lay slack and whose head lolled about with the uncontrolled movements of a rag doll. Rex was not the first person to be surprised at the speed with which a man can die when the windpipe is constricted.

He felt weak as he staggered to his feet. Not the weakness arising out of physical effort alone, but also because of emotional strain.

Throughout the duel, there had been hope at the back of his mind. Hope that before it was over help would come from the barracks. But there was no sign of help.

He looked round him.

The mob was closing in on him. Silently. But with ghastly and inevitable purpose. They were going to tear him apart. Literally. When they had finished with him, his limbs would be wrenched from his body.

Resistance? It was useless. Futile. Like trying to resist the course of the stars or the movements of the tides.

Yet, because there is something basically illogical about man, Rex looked swiftly about for his discarded bayonet. It was not to be seen. Either it was concealed among those countless feet, or it had been picked up as a trophy.

He wondered about Pete. The last time he had seen Pete was when the Englishman had been moving towards Monclaire. Rex looked over the sea of turbaned heads.

Suddenly, in the distance, those heads seemed to coalesce and then divide. A roar went up from them. A roar of helpless anger. It spread and was taken up by the Arabs near to Rex.

A bugle sounded. The notes were thin and indescribably lovely. It was a legion bugle. And he saw the *kepis*. Blue and white Legion *kepis*. Hundreds of them, driving like a spear through the mob.

And already the Arabs were retreating along the Rue St. Jean. It began slowly, reluctantly. But within a minute they were running.

They pushed against him. They almost knocked him down. But he was scarcely aware of the fact. He knew only relief mixed with anxiety. The relief was personal and natural. The anxiety was for the rest of the section — particularly Pete. And Monclaire, too. For, although a wide military gulf divided them, Rex shared a general, feeling of respect for his company officer.

When the street was clear, he saw them. Saw all of them. They were battered. Their uniforms were torn. Most of them had lost their rifles. But they were alive and not greatly harmed.

Pete reached him first. His usually immaculate fair hair was flopping over his forehead. His face was bruised. But he was smiling. And there was something ineffably comforting in that clipped and cultured English voice. That cynically imperturbable voice which said after he had glanced at the strangled Arab: 'I say, old man, have you been quarrelling again?'

In spite of his exhaustion, Rex grinned.

'Yep. That guy and me just didn't get along so well together . . . Say, where's Annice?'

'We've lost her. She broke away from Monclaire. I tried to help him, but that damned mob stopped me getting any-where near. I doubt if we'll ever find her now.'

★ ★ ★

Major Baya, the staff adjutant, had brought out the relief column, which comprised the whole duty company. For him it had been a most satisfactory morning. Monclaire (of whom he was intensely jealous) had caused a riot in the middle of Sadazi. And he, Baya, had retrieved the situation . . .

There was going to be a lot of eyebrow-raising when a report of this reached the staff at Algiers. That drunken fool Jeux would be finished. And Monclaire would certainly face a stringent inquiry. Already, Baya could see himself as the new Colonel Commandant at Dini Sadazi.

Monclaire formed his section at the rear of the column for the short return march to barracks. Then he strode up to the front and saluted Baya.

Major Baya returned the salute slowly

— expressing calculated contempt. Monclaire said evenly: 'Is every man returning to barracks?'

'*Oui*. The mob is dispersed, is it not? You have nothing more to fear, *capitaine*.'

Monclaire coloured slightly.

'The trouble is by no means over, major. Unless the streets are patrolled we may have new riots.'

Major Baya smiled thinly.

'I will put the point to the colonel.'

'Surely it would be better to make arrangements immediately.'

'You concern yourself too much, *capitaine*. You must forgive me if I no longer have complete faith in your judgment of these matters.'

Monclaire shrugged his shoulders. His face was dark with fury as he returned to his section.

But Baya was well pleased. He was no fool, was Baya. He knew well enough that Monclaire's advice was good. But, he told himself, a little more trouble in Sadazi would make doubly sure that Major Baya was soon gazetted Colonel Baya . . .

And, as they approached the barracks,

99

those words of Monclaire's were more than confirmed.

Sullen crowds of Arabs watched them.

There was a sound of hissing. Once, a stone was thrown, hitting a legionnaire on the shoulder. The atmosphere was poisoned with hate.

6

The Wreckage

Colonel Jeux poured himself another brandy. Then he said to Monclaire: 'But what am I to do? I am under orders to send a company to Tutana tomorrow. Yet we are threatened with civil disturbances here and I dare not deplete the garrison ... *Dieu*! What is the answer?'

Two hours had passed since the street riot. Monclaire, who had regretfully changed into his best service kit, stared moodily out of the window. He said tentatively: 'You could wireless a request to Algiers for reinforcements.'

Jeux banged down the empty glass. He had taken just enough drink to stimulate his brain into fuddled activity.

'I dare not do that! Algiers would want to know what's been happening. There would be an inquiry ... I would be asked to resign ... '

'But you've got to tell them. You can't ignore a situation like this in a report. That would be a court martial offence.'

Jeux let out a low groan. He slumped behind his desk. Then he said: 'I know . . . I know . . . But I — I thought that if I could deal with the situation myself first, it would not look so bad. Algiers would not worry so much about a civil commotion which had already been dealt with.'

'But, colonel, when I leave with my company for Tutana tomorrow, you will be at only two-thirds your normal strength. It is quite inadequate for keeping the peace in Sadazi with things as they are. And remember this — there is a European civil population here. You are responsible for their safety. There is also that cursed woman, Annice Tovak. Her disappearance is an international matter. It will have to be reported to her government — and from what I know of the Czech government, they will not let an opportunity like this go by. They will get all the propaganda they can out of it.'

'Then we must make another attempt to bring her in.'

Monclaire pursed his lips. He was glad his back was turned to the colonel. This was like arguing with a frightened child.

'We would be massacred. We would have no chance among those narrow streets, no matter how many men went out. Anyway — I doubt if she is in Sadazi now. She obviously has found favour with the Arabs, and I don't doubt that they have removed her.'

He turned and faced Jeux. And as he did so, Monclaire felt a surge of overwhelming pity for the man. He was helpless. Jeux knew he was helpless. He was finished. Jeux knew he was finished.

Unless . . .

Monclaire said gently: 'There is a possible way out, *mon colonel*. I can delay leaving for Tutana for twenty-four hours, perhaps. It need not affect the time of our arrival, for we can make it up with forced marches.'

Jeux regarded him blankly. Then gradually the meaning percolated his brain.

'Ah *oui*. It would keep the garrison at

full strength for an extra day.'

'Precisely — and if there is any trouble, I think it will occur within the next few hours. If my company stays, we ought to be able to deal with it.'

Jeux's face creased into lines of puerile joy. Then anxiety returned.

'But Algiers . . . '

'Wireless an outline report to Algiers immediately. Say that a European woman has deliberately disappeared, and there have been minor disturbances. I will write it for you, if you wish. Then, when everything has settled down, and my company has left for Tutana, you can send another message reporting the exact sequence of events — but missing out the fact that the column for Tutana was delayed.'

Jeux nodded vigorously. The clouds were lifting. He groped for the brandy bottle.

'It is good. I knew I could rely on you, *mon ami*.'

He concentrated upon the alcohol.

But Monclaire felt strained and unhappy as he left Jeux's office and walked towards the mess. The decision to hold his company in Sadazi would certainly improve the garrison's chances of dealing with further violence. But it was a flagrant breach of discipline.

And the wireless message he was about to send . . .

It would be deliberately misleading because it would not contain all the facts. It would not mention that Arabs had been killed that morning in Rue St. Jean. Or that the column was not leaving for Tutana according to orders.

And there was another dismal aspect. Colonel Jeux took the ultimate responsibility for all this. But he, Monclaire, had suggested it to him. If anything went wrong . . .

Monclaire tried to console himself with the thought that he had been morally compelled to do something for Jeux, who was obviously incapable of doing much for himself.

He entered the sparsely furnished mess lounge. There he hoped to be able to compose the wireless message in reasonable privacy and comfort. At this time the other officers were usually on duty. It was annoying, therefore, to find that Major Baya was there.

Baya was sitting at a writing table, his pen poised thoughtfully. He gave Monclaire one of his distant nods.

Monclaire was about to pass when he saw the slip of paper on the desk. It had a printed heading. It read: Legion Etrangere. It was a radio cipher form. And on it, in large capital letters, Baya had written: *'Urgent. To Military Secretary, High Command, Algiers . . .'*

He was not able to see the rest, for Baya hastily covered the slip with his arm. His plump, moon-like face glared at Monclaire.

He said: 'Do you make a habit of reading other officers' correspondence, *capitaine?'*

Monclaire ignored the rhetorical question. He said softly: 'I gather you are making a report about today's events, major?'

Baya was the type of man who frequently resorted to blustering. He tried it now . . .

'I refuse to discuss a matter which does not concern you. You are being most insolent, and I . . . '

Monclaire cut in smoothly: 'I think it does concern me, major. You have no right whatever to send an official message to Algiers without first being instructed to do so by the commanding officer.'

'*Le demon!* Are you instructing me, the adjutant, on my duties? I shall not tolerate it!'

He had risen from the table, the better to express his indignation. In doing so, he had uncovered the cipher slip.

Monclaire picked it up. Baya tried to snatch it, but Monclaire turned away. A few seconds sufficed to read the rest of the message. It gave a detailed and highly colourful account of the riots, and of Annice Tovak. It suggested that the riots were caused because of incompetence on Monclaire's part, rather than because of the influence of the woman on an ignorant and inflamed mob. It implied, with some subtlety, that only decisive action by Baya had restored order. And it ended by stating — with truth — that

Colonel Jeux was incapable of exercising his command because of excessive drinking. He, Baya, requested permission to take over immediately, pending other arrangements.

It was a masterpiece. A perfect example of the art of blending hard facts with evil distortions. It would be most difficult to disprove.

Monclaire screwed the slip into a compact ball and flicked it onto the floor.

'You had better not send this,' he said.

Baya ceased to bluster. He contrived a caricature of a smile.

'I can understand your concern, *capitaine*. The message will make matters very difficult for you.'

'I'm not thinking of myself, major. I can answer for my own actions. But Colonel Jeux can not. Your message would ruin him.'

'He deserves to be ruined ... incompetent, drunken imbecile!'

'Yes — he's a drunkard, and I don't doubt he's incompetent. But it was not always so. He has become what he is because he has served France too long

108

and too faithfully. It would be a poor reward to betray him now.'

Baya sat down again. He looked thoughtful. Then he said slowly: 'You're altruistic, *capitaine*. I admire you for it, but such unselfish loyalty — it is foolish. Can't you see that Jeux cannot last much longer, in any case? What difference does it make if he goes now or later . . . except; perhaps, to us . . . '

He paused to stare with a calculated intensity at Monclaire. He added: 'Maybe I have been unreasonable where you personally are concerned. Suppose — suppose we come to an agreement?'

Monclaire did not answer the implied question. But his face expressed genuine curiosity. Baya continued with increasing confidence.

'I am thinking that I could rewrite the message to Algiers, cutting out any criticism of you. In fact, I could say your conduct today was excellent. Then, with Jeux removed and I in command; much could be done for you, Monclaire. I could . . . '

'*Batard!*'

Monclaire breathed the expletive through still lips. Baya looked startled.

'*Capitaine!* I cannot tolerate such an insult. Please remember that I am your senior officer.'

'I cannot forget the fact. It disgusts me. You will understand that I will not join in any such filthy deal. Such things may be normal among politicians, but they are not becoming to soldiers.'

'Your decision is final?'

'Completely final.'

Baya stooped and retrieved the crumpled cipher slip.

He said: 'Then I am sending the message as it stands.'

Monclaire's eyebrows had lowered.

'You are determined on that?'

'*Oui.* I will be frank with you, *capitaine.* You see, this is my opportunity and it could have been yours. I am not going to let it slip by.'

Monclaire regarded Baya thoughtfully. Outwardly, he appeared tense but calm. Within him, Monclaire's brain was seething.

Baya's message would produce serious results. But, as yet, Baya did not know all the facts. What would happen when he discovered the decision to delay the departure for Tutana? Baya would certainly report the fact in another signal to Algiers. And, as a result, Jeux would be put under arrest . . .

It would be useless to explain to the High Command that the delay need not affect the arrival time. Useless to tell them of the plan to march a little longer each day so as to make up for the lost twenty-four hours.

For, in the Legion — as in any efficient army — an order had the status of a divine edict. An order must be obeyed implicitly. And for an obvious reason — if those who gave orders could not be certain that they would be carried out exactly in every detail, any coordinated strategy would be impossible.

And as for Monclaire himself . . .

As he assessed the situation, Monclaire admitted that he probably had many faults, both as a soldier and as a man. But he had always tried to conduct himself with distinction. And he had had more than his share of active service. Yet promotion had been slow. Perhaps that was because during long years in the desert, he had not been able to make those influential contacts at headquarters. While he had been risking his skin, officers like Baya had been feathering their military nests at the base.

Yet, despite all its injustices, Monclaire loved the life. It was the only life. Any other would be intolerable.

And now it was threatened with ruin by an ambitious and unscrupulous swine . . .

He looked down at the bald circle at the top of Baya's head. He watched the plump and shapeless hands smoothing out that damned radio signal . . .

In a few seconds, Baya would strut out of the mess. He would turn left and walk along the corridor to the wireless room. There he would give it to the operator for Morse transmission to Algiers . . .

Then it would all be finished.

And for what purpose? For the greater glory of Major Baya. That was all.

It was not in Monclaire's character to plead before any man. But he felt tempted to do so now. He was restrained only by the knowledge that such an appeal would be useless. Suddenly Monclaire felt very tired and very bitter. He watched Baya fold the cipher slip neatly, and put it in his tunic pocket. He watched him turn towards the door.

And he saw Baya stop, as though paralysed, and gaze blankly across the room.

Monclaire turned to follow his line of vision.

Colonel Jeux was in the doorway.

He was leaning against the wall, a thin smile on his lined face. He returned Baya's gaze for several long moments.

Then Jeux said: 'I heard, Major. I ought to have guessed that you would try something like this . . . '

He took a few steps towards them. They were slightly unsteady steps. The movement eased the tension. Baya gave a short laugh. Obviously it was intended to indicate an untroubled conscience, but it was not convincing.

'*Mon colonel*, I am glad you have come. I was about to speak to you in your office. You . . . '

'Don't lie, major. I've just told you — I've heard enough to know what you were about to do. I think I can guess what was in the message you were going to send. But I would like to read it. Give it to me!'

'You — you're mistaken, *mon colonel*. And the message . . . it is of no importance. I can explain if . . . '

'Give it to me — '

There was something surprising about the way Jeux repeated the order.

All his former flabby indecision had gone. The words were snapped out with harsh and utter finality. And his posture, too, had changed. Suddenly he was erect again. The body tense and strong. The mouth a thin unrelenting line. The eyes steady and cold.

Watching him, Monclaire felt a surge of surprise and gladness. He recalled reading somewhere that when great nations are in their decline they always — just once — achieve something that is a flashback to their former glories. Could it not be so with individual men, too? Was it not happening now to Jeux? Yes, it was.

For here was the almost forgotten Jeux. The Jeux who had existed before brandy had rotted his mind.

Temporarily, at least, the travail of the years had been lifted from him. It had needed the lash of betrayal and humiliation to do it. But it had been done.

And Baya obviously realised that he was no longer confronted by a drunken fool. He shuffled uncomfortably. As though under a mesmeric compulsion, his hand went to his tunic pocket

But, with an effort, he restrained it half way.

'I cannot hand over the message here, colonel. I — I will do so in your office, where I can explain privately.'

'Don't bother. You have told me enough. Major Baya, you will not have the opportunity to send any messages of any sort to Algiers. I will give orders that only signals bearing my signature are to be transmitted.'

Baya's face contused to a deep red.

'I cannot accept that. I am the adjutant and . . . '

'You are no longer adjutant. You are

relieved of all duties.'

'You have no power to do that. You will have to make a recommendation to the High Command first.'

'I shall make my recommendation, major. And it will be approved. But meantime my decision stands.'

Like most crafty men, Baya was prone to bursts of hysteria when duplicity failed. He produced one now. His words rushed out in an uncontrolled verbal torrent.

'You will suffer for this, colonel . . . Algiers will know what's been happening here . . . I'll tell them there's been slaughter in the streets today because of Monclaire's stupidity. I'll tell them that the garrison is commanded by a drunkard . . . Yes . . . a drunkard! That's what you are, and it's time you were told . . . '

Jeux thumbed open the cover of his holster. He extracted his pistol and aimed the heavy weapon at Baya's chest. As Baya saw it he lapsed into astonished silence.

'That's enough, major. You are under arrest for insubordination!'

Baya's breathing became audible. He

spoke with difficulty — in contrast to his previous vituperation.

'You — you are going much too far, colonel. I have work to do. Perhaps we will talk again when you are in a more reasonable mood . . . '

He attempted to push past Jeux. But Jeux's pistol, pushed into direct contact with Baya's chest, brought him to a halt.

Baya glared at the barrel. He was almost sobbing with fury. It was his fury that killed him,

He whipped up his left hand in an attempt to brush the gun away.

It was a badly judged attempt. Instead of hitting the side of the gun, Baya struck directly beneath the breech. It jerked up. The effect was to force the trigger against Jeux's forefinger.

There was a hollow, echoing explosion. And an immediate odour of burned cordite.

Major Baya lay stretched on the floor. The grey remnants of his cerebral organs were oozing out of his skull and over his face.

It was Monclaire who took over. Never

before had Monclaire thought and acted with such speed.

He said: *'Permittez-moi,'* and took away Jeux's still smoking pistol. He placed that pistol in Baya's hand, folding the dead fingers around the butt. Then he dropped Baya's own pistol into the colonel's holster.

There was just time to remove the cipher message from Baya's pocket before the orderly officer and two N.C.O.s came rushing into the mess.

'Suicide,' Monclaire told them as they stood aghast. 'Another second and we might have been able to stop it. He fired as we were coming in . . . '

★ ★ ★

The medical officer was a newly commissioned young man. He blended tedious enthusiasm for his work with awe-struck respect for all senior officers. He almost saluted Baya's blanket-covered corpse as it was carried out.

Then he blinked anxiously at Monclaire through horn spectacles.

'I say — why do you think he did it?' he asked.

Monclaire was in no mood for a hypothetical discussion with a *sous lieutenant*.

'Possibly because he was tired of life.'

The medical officer nodded seriously.

'Ah, *oui*. But . . . but I am surprised that he should come into the mess to kill himself. I mean . . . his own room would be a more natural place.'

Monclaire felt a strong desire to order the youthful doctor out of the room. But he restrained himself. He said curtly: 'I agree, it is unusual. But one could always rely on Major Baya to do something out of the ordinary.'

'And he was not a very good shot, was he?'

'Why?'

'Well *capitaine*, he blew the top of his head away, and the bullet was obviously moving in an upward direction. As it happened, he was killed instantly, but he could easily have lingered for many hours. Why didn't he place the gun level against his forehead? That would be a much easier thing to do.'

Monclaire pulled out his cigarette case. He offered it to the medical officer, who accepted with respectful alacrity.

When they were smoking, Monclaire said: 'I think it must have been a sudden decision. Probably he decided to get it over when he heard the colonel and me approaching. In his haste he would not have time to aim properly.'

The medical officer nodded vigorously.

'*Mais oui*! Now you mention it, it is all so obvious . . . *merci, capitaine*. Now, if you'll excuse me, I will make out my formal report.'

And a fully satisfied *sous lieutenant* departed for the medical inspection room.

Monclaire finished his cigarette. Then he walked towards Jeux's office. He had managed to ease Jeux out of the mess within a few minutes of Baya's death. For the colonel had stood dumb and palsied during that hectic period and Monclaire had feared for him. Feared that he might blurt out the truth.

He was only dimly aware of distant

sounds of shouting as he crossed the parade ground. In a disconnected way he realised that the noise came from the town centre, and probably the Arabs were already causing trouble. But the conclusion made no impact on his mind. At the moment he was concerned only with Jeux . . .

And the moment he entered the office he knew that his fears were confirmed.

Jeux was half sitting in his chair, half sprawled across his desk. An empty brandy bottle lay upturned at his elbow and a tumbler was beside it. He looked up slowly, as though the action of raising his head was an effort.

And he whispered: '*Dieu* . . . I've murdered him . . . '

Monclaire put his arms under Jeux's shoulders. He lifted him back into the chair.

'You did nothing of the sort. Baya killed himself as surely as if he had pressed the trigger. So far as you are concerned, it was a something for which you were not responsible.'

'Then I must tell the truth.'

'The truth would serve no purpose — other than to do Baya's work even after his death. Don't you see? Everything would emerge at the inquiry. Yes, perhaps in the end we would be formally vindicated. But only formally. What sort of career would we have after such a scandal? We would be finished, *mon colonel*, finished . . . '

Jeux raised a shaking hand and pressed it to his temple.

'But I can't go on . . . *non*, I can't . . . '

He began to sob. Silently. Inwardly. But none the less obviously.

That brief flashback had vanished for ever. The real Colonel Jeux, the brave and determined soldier of France, had re-emerged for only those few brief minutes in the mess. Now he had reverted again.

But Monclaire felt a deep gratitude. Gratitude for the fact that he had been able to glimpse, temporarily, those qualities that had once, long ago, been there permanently. And he also felt a hard, unyielding desire to protect this old soldier. To defend him from himself.

He spoke firmly and with a confidence

122

he was far from feeling.

'Listen, *mon colonel*, we are friends are we not? Then I want you to trust me. You are tired. You must rest. Now that Baya's dead, I am the second in command here. I want you to leave it all, leave everything to me. I have faced crises before and I can face this one. I will settle the trouble in Sadazi within a day. I will find that damned woman, Annice Tovak, and have her sent back to Oran where she can do no more harm. Then I will go out to Tutana to patrol the oil line, and none will know that there has been any delay. Will you trust me?'

At first Jeux did not answer. He stared blankly at Monclaire. Then he murmured: 'You can do no worse than I, *mon ami*. I will do as you say. I will rest for a day. And I will confirm any orders you give . . .'

He rose and swayed.

He took a reeling and circuitous route to the filing cabinet. With fumbling fingers he opened the 'Miscellaneous' drawer. There he found a fresh bottle of brandy. Clutching it, he shuffled out of the office.

★ ★ ★

Monclaire sat in the vacated chair. He drew a note pad towards him and wrote down the problems that confronted him. In that way, they became clear. But they also became even more overwhelming.

It was now nearly five o'clock in the afternoon. In almost exactly twelve hours a company was due to leave to protect the Tutana oil line. But the company could not leave because serious trouble might flare up in the town, and the garrison would have to be at full strength to deal with it.

But it would be worse than useless to explain this to the High Command. Their concern was the oil line. And they would expect their orders for its protection to be followed to the most minute detail.

Obviously, the Touaregs had their agitators working in Sadazi. And it was those agitators who were organising the mass hysteria, perhaps using the Czech woman as a pawn.

If he could strike first? If he could pull

in the leaders and make an example of a few of them?

A tinkling of broken glass.

It interrupted Monclaire's thoughts. It was carried faintly but clearly on the afternoon air.

Then Monclaire realised that there had been other sounds in his ears, too. But he had been too absorbed to heed them. They were a cacophony of many voices. And they were getting louder.

Monclaire crossed to the window.

The barracks were surrounded by tall iron rails, and the main gates faced him. The stone guardroom stood beside the open gates. And there one of the windows was broken, the glass glittering on the ground.

But the main point of interest was immediately outside the rails. There, a mob of several hundred Arabs had gathered, and their numbers were growing fast.

Monclaire saw the massive figure of Sergeant Zatov, the N.C.O. in charge of the guard. Zatov had drawn his twelve men in a single line facing the mob. But he had made no attempt to close the gates. In this he was right, for the Arabs were making no attempt to rush the barracks. And any premature precaution would look bad. It would merely suggest panic.

The office door opened. A slightly built and rather pallid lieutenant entered and saluted.

Monclaire recognised Gina, the orderly officer of the day.

Gina's eyes roved the room, as though searching for Jeux. Then he said: 'B Company is at readiness in case of trouble, *capitaine.*'

Monclaire nodded.

'Keep them inside the building. I don't want to anticipate trouble. Have you any idea . . . '

Gina interrupted. He was gazing over Monclaire's shoulder and through the window.

'*Capitaine!* Look!'

Monclaire wheeled round.

The mob had parted to let three people through. The trio were walking quietly and confidently through the gates. There

126

they were intercepted by Zatov. After a few seconds, Zatov escorted them into the guardroom.

Monclaire and Gina looked at each other in bewilderment.

Two of the trio were Touaregs. The other was Annice Tovak.

★ ★ ★

The guardroom was linked to the commandant's office by an aged and battery operated telephone. This gave an uncertain ring, and Monclaire pressed the instrument to his ear. Zatov's voice came rustily through. But his excitement was easily detectable.

He said: 'That woman is here, *capitaine*, and . . .'

'I know. Bring them here.'

'That's what they want, *capitaine*. They are here to see the colonel.'

Monclaire slapped down the receiver. He was tempted to go back to the window, but decided not to do so. After dismissing Gina — who would certainly have preferred to stay — he sat at the desk and waited.

The room seemed strangely empty as Monclaire waited. As though it were a vacuum straining to be filled. And the minutes went by heavily, reluctantly. Deliberately, he suppressed the teeming questions that tried to form in his brain. They would, he told himself, be answered soon enough.

Clong!

The barracks clock struck the hour.

And the door opened.

Annice Tovak was there.

She glided past the massive Sergeant Zatov. The two Arabs followed. Monclaire recognised one of them as Tu el Adaa, in whose house Annice had been found. But he gave him no more than a brief glance, then concentrated again on Annice. And, because he was a Frenchman, he thought: '*Mon Dieu*, no wonder Legionnaire Tovak tried to desert to reach her! She's beautiful. Why did I not notice it before? Perhaps I am getting old . . . '

She justified his silent praise.

Despite the fact that her linen dress was now rumpled and a little torn.

128

Despite the fact that her vivid fair hair was astray and untended. Despite the tension, which made her face hard, and turned her blue eyes into cold seas.

They advanced on the desk, she leading. Monclaire rose and gestured towards the only other chair in the room. She ignored it. He sat down again, a little uncomfortably.

Her voice had the unnatural clarity of an amplified whisper. She said: 'We want to see the commanding officer.'

'I am the commanding officer for the time being. The colonel is — unwell. And I want to speak with you, *madame*. Do you realise that you were the indirect cause of this morning's bloodshed? Have you forgotten that you escaped while under arrest?'

She stood very still. She looked over Monclaire's head and into the middle distance as she answered.

'I am not interested, *capitaine*.'

'You ought to be — for now you are here, I am having you deported from French Morocco.'

The fat Adaa was standing on Annice's

right. His staring eyes reflected faint amusement. The other Touareg — richly robed, like Adaa — was less subtle. He smiled openly. He even made a gesture towards his knife.

Monclaire added sharply: 'And these Touareg associates are also under arrest. I have no doubt they have been of assistance to you.'

She said: 'None of us is under arrest, *capitaine*.' There was a quiet finality in her words as she added: 'And I am not leaving Morocco.'

'*Oui?* You interest me, *madame*.'

'I thought I would. I have had experience of fighting armed tyranny such as yours, *capitaine*. During the war I was a saboteur against the Nazis. I think my knowledge will prove useful now. I have willingly placed it at the disposal of the Arab peoples.'

Monclaire had difficulty in disguising his mounting fury. To compare the French administration of her African colonies with the jackboot methods of the Nazi, was more than he could stand.

But he said: 'I have heard of your war

experiences. The matter was referred to during the court martial of your husband.'

Her skin, always pale, became paler still. For just a moment, the reference to Legionnaire Tovak put her off balance. She gave herself time to recover before saying: 'Knowing my background, and knowing what you did to my husband, you will understand why I am glad to help in the struggle against the French . . . '

She took a long step forward, and placed her small clenched fists on the desk. Then she added slowly: 'Tyranny is the same, whatever name you give it, *monsieur capitaine*. I risked my life before in fighting it, and I am doing so again. The Touaregs have told me how the French use their Legion lackeys to terrorise their lands, to thwart their right to self-government. And I, *capitaine*, have told them how to meet terror with terror . . .

'I have told them that everywhere the Western oppression of the coloured races is waning. In any one place it needs only courage and ruthless action to end it. And it can be ended here in Sadazi . . .

'*Capitaine, you will have to evacuate this entire garrison by midnight!*'

Monclaire gazed at her unbelievingly. As he fumbled for a cigarette he thought: 'She's mad! Quite mad!'

But before he could speak, she said: 'No, I have not lost my reason. I know exactly what I am doing in all its implications. Once the Legion leaves Sadazi it can never return, for your prestige will have suffered too great a blow. And it will be impossible to run the oil lines through Touareg territory, for without this base they cannot be.'

Monclaire drew cigarette smoke deep into his lungs, He wondered what kind of preposterous reasoning had led the woman to think she could compel the docile retreat of a garrison of more than four hundred men.

He said smoothly: 'You fascinate me, *madame*. Please continue.'

She turned towards the window.

'Look out here, *capitaine*.'

He rose from behind the desk and did so. He saw the hard stretch of the parade ground. He saw the guard drawn before the gates. And he saw the mob beyond the gates — a much larger mob now, and more noisy, but still not making any serious trouble.

'You are not looking in the right direction, *capitaine*. See . . . '

She was pointing beyond the Arabs and slightly to the left of them. He was puzzled. He saw only the distant and shabby façade of a familiar building.

'There's only the hotel there, *madame*.'

'And who live in the hotel?'

He glanced at her cautiously.

'European residents, mostly. Also a few tourists who are stupid enough to make a camel trek out here. But you know that.'

'Yes, I know. But I'll be more precise. There are twenty-two white people in the *Hotel Afrique* at this moment, including eight women and five children.'

'I'm aware of it.'

'And the hotel has just been occupied by a strong force of armed Touaregs. Were you aware of that?'

Tobacco smoke caught in his throat. He coughed compulsively and was ashamed at the betrayal of emotion. When he had recovered, he said, as casually as he could: 'Then they will soon be put out of the hotel. And they will be answerable to a military court. That hotel is reserved to white residents.'

'Your knowledge of recent events is as outmoded as your conception of racial privileges, *monsieur capitaine*. You see, the entire twenty-two residents are prisoners of the Touareg people. They are confined to the hotel . . .

'And, *capitaine*, understand this — unless the garrison quit Sadazi by midnight they will be killed! All of them will die. The women and the children, perhaps, will die quickly. The men may be less fortunate.'

Her words were delivered without special emphasis. They came as an indisputable statement of fact. Like a simple mathematical equation.

Monclaire felt her eyes upon him. He turned to meet the challenge. She was smiling. But, by some weird physical perversion, the smile had taken away her beauty. It was transitory, but it was nonetheless ghastly. Monclaire felt a desire to shudder. Suddenly she had become the negation of all that was traditionally implied by the term woman.

He said: 'If you have really been so wicked as to mislead the Arabs into taking such a course, then you will pay dearly, Madame Tovak. And so will the Arabs. It will be a matter of a few moments for me to send a patrol to the hotel to ensure the safety of the Europeans.'

Monclaire moved back towards the desk. His hand went out to the handbell there. He intended to send for Lieutenant Gina and give the necessary orders immediately.

But her voice stopped him.

She said: 'If you do that, the Europeans will be killed immediately. They will be killed before your wretched patrol has left the barracks. And their bodies will be spiked on your barrack railings for all to see.'

A paralysis seized Monclaire. It froze and made useless each bodily muscle. His hand remained outstretched. It was as though he were posing in a grotesque charade. Only gradually did mobility return. And only after deliberate effort. A heavy drum beat in his brain. It thumped out a message that said: '*It's the truth . . . it's the truth . . .* '

He knew that she was not lying. No woman could speak that way under the impetus of an empty threat.

Slowly, very slowly, he went to the chair. He slumped heavily into it. He stared at Sergeant Zatov, who was standing beside the door. The focal point of his vision was Zatov's red beard. But he did not see either the beard or the man. He saw twenty-two civilians, eight of them women and five children, who were on the brink of being butchered. They were civilians for whose safety he, as acting commandant, was responsible.

He saw just how easy it must have been for this crazy but well educated woman to have imposed her satanic plan upon illiterate and semi-literate Arabs,

He saw how the cruel strokes of fate had helped to serve her purpose. That scene in the wineshop, which must have immediately become a sensation among the native population. The maltreatment

136

of her in Rue St. Jean, which was witnessed by hundreds. The consequent riot in which many Arabs were killed and maimed. All this, added to the already existing unrest over the Tutana oil line, made fertile ground for one who was skilled m the craft of undercover warfare.

And it had started less than thirty-six hours before with the execution of Legionnaire Tovak. Damn Tovak! He was an insignificant fellow. He was a very frightened fellow. Yet this woman had loved him so much that she was ready to stir the cauldrons of hell to avenge his death.

She was speaking again. Her voice came from far off, as if he were listening to words spoken in a nightmare. She was saying: 'I see that you understand me, *capitaine*. The garrison has no choice. It must leave — for I'm sure you would not want the death of so many innocents upon your hands . . .'

Monclaire turned his head towards her. Suddenly, his brain cleared. He cursed himself for allowing it to become dazed under shock. He had overlooked the obvious master card that he held. But he saw it now.

He said: '*Oui*, I understand you very well I also know that without your influence the Arabs of Sadazi could never have conceived such evil. And without your presence, they will be lost. They are to be deprived of that presence. As I said when you first entered this room, you are under arrest. But I am not sending you to Oran for deportation. You are far too dangerous. I am holding you here, in a cell, while I prepare a report for Algiers. Further action will rest with the High Command there, but I have no doubt that it will be drastic and . . . '

The corpse of Major Baya was recalled to his mind.

Baya had died because he had wanted to give Algiers the full facts of the day's riots — and more. It was vital that the Command did not know anything until the trouble had been settled. Yet, if Annice Tovak were handed over to them, the full and awful story of the riot would be revealed. There would be no chance of playing it down. And they would know that the order to depart for Tutana had been ignored . . .

'You are worried, *capitaine*?'

Her tones mocked him as they cut across his thoughts. She added: 'Perhaps you have realised that my version of what happened today would not reflect much credit on you?'

He started. She laughed.

'No, *capitaine*, I am not psychic. And I do not possess secret information. It is just an obvious deduction, isn't it? But the question will not arise. Before we came into the barracks we gave very precise orders for our safety.'

He did not need to be told. He knew now what they were.

'You mean . . . the civilians in the hotel . . . ,'

'But exactly! If we — all three of us — do not leave here unharmed by sundown, half of the Europeans will die. The others will remain alive while you reconsider your position. It would be better to let us go, *capitaine* . . . '

For the second time that afternoon Monclaire knew absolute defeat. He thought that perhaps it was because he was fighting on unfamiliar ground. In a conflict of guns between armed men he was equal to most situations. The military arts had become almost elementary to him. He could foresee an enemy's tactical deployments. He was seldom at a loss for the correct counter-move.

But this . . .

This was not an open fight. This was a fight in which the politics of blackmail, barbaric hate and shadowy subterfuge were the main factors. And in which the lives of innocent and helpless people had become the enemy's bastion.

The evacuation of Sadazi?

Unthinkable. As well as making impossible the protection of the oil line, such a retreat might easily strike a deathblow at the entire French Colonial Empire. Under such a loss of prestige there would be unrest and uprisings throughout the African possessions from the Cameroons to Tunisia.

Let the Europeans be massacred?

Equally unthinkable. Every decent human instinct revoked at the thought of several hundred soldiers cowering in a barracks while civilians were being killed a few hundred yards away. And, since many of the civilians were foreign nationals visiting Sadazi with tourist permits, the result would be widespread international complications.

Somehow, in some way, the Europeans had to be rescued before they could be harmed.

But how?

In God's name how, when the first move out of the barracks would be a signal for the Touaregs to knife their hostages . . . ?

She had moved towards the door, her Arab escort behind her. But Zatov was barring the way. He gestured to Zatov, and the big Russian moved clear with obvious reluctance.

At the open door, Annice Tovak turned. She was beautiful again. As a malignant growth can have repellant beauty.

She said: 'You will be hoping to find an answer between now and midnight, *capitaine*. Hope, if you wish, but you will be wasting time. You will have to leave

Sadazi. And in return, the lives of the Europeans will be spared . . . Remember, no help can reach you in time. And your garrison is captive in their own barracks — until they decide to go for good. *Bonsoir, capitaine . . .* '

She was gone.

He was alone again.

And her last words had been the most cruel of all. She had said that help could not reach him in time. That was true. It would be useless to wireless for assistance. The nearest reinforcements were two hundred miles away. But it would have made no difference if they had been at the gates of the town. Those twenty-two people would die before anything could be done for them.

And she had said the garrison was captive in its own barracks. True again! In the whole long story of the world's soldiers, had there ever been one who had found himself in such a ghastly impasse as this?

Never, Monclaire decided. Never.

He stood up. Through the window he saw her and the two Touaregs walking out of the gates. The mob was cheering them.

The sound of a bugle mixed with the cheers. He looked towards the flag mast. The bugle was playing as the Tricolour came down at the end of the day.

He wondered if it would ascend the mast at dawn.

Suddenly Monclaire's face hardened. His fist closed involuntarily round the butt of his pistol.

He spoke aloud, but he spoke to himself. And he was looking at the now bare mast as he said: 'I swear before all the glories of France that the Tricolour shall rise again — and these people shall not die . . . '

7

Mission for Two

Clong!

The hour has struck. Which hour? Look up and see. For the clock at Sadazi warns, but it does not tell.

Six hours to midnight.

Why not say six o'clock?

Because it is only midnight that matters. It is at midnight when the satanic ultimatum expires . . .

★   ★   ★

Twenty-two Europeans heard it. The sullen stroke came faintly to them through the roof of the hotel cellar that was their prison. The small and now stifling cellar into which — bewildered, protesting, frightened and unbelieving, according to character — they had been herded.

The men looked at their watches.

Then suddenly they resumed their talk, all speaking but none heeding.

' . . . two hours in this place. It's an outrage . . . '

' . . . of course, they'll be shot for this. The French have pretty sound ideas about colonial government . . . '

' . . . always suffered from asthma, and this is making it worse. I'll certainly put in a claim for damages . . . '

' . . . if I had my way . . . '

The women were less vocal. They sat on the stone floor.

And from that unlikely position, some tried to assume attitudes of feminine elegance. Others — the more mature — had fallen asleep, propped against the unyielding walls. Only the children were happy. They, with vividly puerile imaginations, saw in their situation only a great and unexpected adventure. They invented boisterous games accordingly.

But all of them — yes, even the children — shared one common emotion. They were confident that soon they would be released from this place. How

145

could it be otherwise? Just as soon as the soldiers heard of what had happened, the doors would be flung open . . .

Ignorance was at least offering comparative comfort.

And Annice Tovak had been wise to insist upon that ignorance. She knew that the prisoners would have been far less docile and confident if they had been told that their lives were being used as the currency to force a bargain.

* * *

Colonel Jeux heard it. But only subconsciously. He slept uneasily upon his bunk. He was fully dressed, even to his boots. And one hand grasped an empty bottle of *Dubouche*, '65.

* * *

Rex and Pete heard it. They, with more than a hundred others of their company, were in their barrack room listening to an excited and fulminating Sergeant Zatov.

Zatov was breaking a military code.

Zatov was describing the interview between Monclaire and Annice Tovak. And since he had witnessed that while in a privileged position, he ought to have kept very quiet about it. But the thought — if it occurred to him — did not worry Zatov in the least. He was being borne upon a crest of irresistible indignation. And since he had to talk to somebody, who better than the men of his company, who were compelled to give him a respectful hearing?

But even if he had been without his rank, Sergeant Zatov would still have had a fascinated audience.

The legionnaires listened to the report with wonder and horror. Like all soldiers of all nations, they often proclaimed their contempt for the army in which they served. But they would not tolerate such opinions from others. They had many times announced that Dini Sadazi was a flea-packed oven and there was no reason to keep a garrison there. If the Arabs wanted the place, well, they were welcome to it. But they felt hard fury when they heard that they might be forced out of the place.

And they had frequently expressed contempt for the handful of over-prosperous and flabby civilians who strutted about the European quarter. They were useless fools who sometimes bought a legionnaire a drink in exchange for some impossible story of military adventure. Or even paid a few francs for the extraordinary privilege of having their photograph taken with one of them, so that the badly developed pictures could in due course be shown to other flabby and slack-mouthed civilians when they got back home.

But the threat to massacre them . . .

That put the civilians on a new and lofty level. Even the most brutalised of the legionnaires — and quite a few of them were that — felt that this ultimatum was an insult to a basic instinct. And a challenge to them, as soldiers.

Because Zatov's command of French was fluent, if grammatically imperfect, all were able to follow at least the outline of his story.

He stood at one end of the barrack room like some gigantic apostle, his beard and his eyes glittering in the fading light.

And when he had at last finished, there was an uneasy stir among the legionnaires. Zatov embraced them all in his malevolent gaze, as though, having taken the trouble to describe an impossible problem, he now had a right to expect an immediate solution.

'Is there nothing you can say?' he demanded after a few moments. 'Have you all lost your tongues as well as your brains?'

Rex was sitting on the comer of his bunk. A newly issued Lebel was across his knees and he had removed the bolt preparatory to drawing a pull-through down the barrel. The cleaning process had been interrupted by Zatov and was entirely forgotten now. He put the encumbrances aside and got to his feet.

When he noticed him, Zatov smiled. And, like all N.C.O.s, he could not resist an attempt at wit.

'Ah,' he said weightily. 'Are we about to receive some more American aid?'

Those who understood laughed immediately. Those who did not follow the international implication also joined the chorus — but after a little delay.

Rex had been long enough in the Legion to know that men like Zatov must be allowed such privileges. He managed a grin.

Then he said: 'I guess we'd all like to know just what's goin' to be done about it. That is — if Annice Tovak wasn't bluffing?'

'Bluffing, you call it. It was no bluff, legionnaire.'

'Then what are we goin' to do?'

Zatov shrugged his huge shoulders.

'I am not in the confidence of the *capitaine*.'

Pete, who had been standing near Rex, pushed slightly forward. He said in his deceptively indifferent voice: 'He hasn't very long to decide, has he? And he hasn't much choice. Either we stay — and the civilians are killed. Or we go.'

'Go! Do you think we're marching out of Sadazi because a hank-haired bitch says so?'

'Then the civilians will die?'

Zatov glared at Pete. And Pete stared pleasantly back. Then, to an accompanying rumble of Slavonic curses, Zatov strode out of the room.

There was an immediate babble of multi-tongued conversation. But neither Rex nor Pete took part in it.

Rex was looking thoughtful as he dragged a small piece of wadding through his rifle. He was showing signs of considerable excitement by the time he had replaced the bolt. A moment later he was tapping Pete on the shoulder. There was never much of an interval between conceiving an idea and acting upon it, where Rex was concerned.

'I'm goin' to ask for an interview with Monclaire,' he said in a fast whisper.

Pete regarded him with composed curiosity.

'Really? But I should hardly think the captain will be in a mood for social discussions with other ranks at this moment. I don't know what's on your mind, but you'd better let it wait, old man.'

'It won't be a social discussion. It'll be about those folks the Touaregs are holding.'

'Ah — I gather you have some ingenious formula for their release?'

At one time, Pete's cynicism had hurt and annoyed Rex. Now he had learned — as many other Americans had learned of Englishmen — that it was merely a protective pose to conceal emotion. Pete belonged to that Saxon school which regarded any display of personal feeling as being slightly reprehensible.

So Rex ignored the remark. He added: 'I've been figuring things out. It seems to me that one man might be able to reach the prisoners without being seen. It wouldn't be like a whole patrol marching out of the barracks.'

'Possibly. And I suppose you see yourself as being the one man. It's most noble of you, old fellow. My congratulations. But what would you do if you did get to the prisoners? Are you proposing to overcome several hundred Touareg thugs single handed and guide the grateful captives to freedom and safety?'

'No, I ain't.'

'Then what?'

'It's this way — I'm thinkin' that those folks are most likely to be locked below ground in one of the cellars. And the guards will be outside the door. Get me?'

Pete nodded.

'I suppose so. A cellar is the logical place, and the guards are not likely to be in with them.'

'Then don't you see? Suppose I could get between the guards and the prisoners! If I was well enough armed, I might be able to hold the Touaregs off while a couple of companies rush the hotel . . . '

He was going to say more, but he broke off because Pete was laughing quietly.

Pete said: 'That, if I may say so, is a typical American conception of tactics. You base your plans upon a wild improbability, then trust to courage and a kindly fate to see you through.'

'Okay, okay. Kill yourself laughing, if you want to. But I guess it's better than doing just nothing. And I guess Monclaire might see it the same way. I'm still going to apply for that interview, and I'm doing it right now.'

Rex began to button his tunic. Then, as he was fastening his *ceinture*, Pete said: 'It's just possible that Monclaire may allow you to attempt something of the sort — but it will only be because he's desperate. If that happens, I cannot possibly permit you to operate alone and unaided. You will require the military experience of the English. Therefore, both of us will request an interview.'

* * *

Monclaire listened carefully. He had agreed to see the two legionnaires only because he knew that such applications were seldom made without good reason. And only thoroughly slack officers made difficulties about seeing their men.

It was vastly annoying, of course, to have to deal with such routine matters at this time of absolute crisis. At a time when he felt that his brain must burst in its efforts to find a solution . . .

But it was typical of the man that from the very beginning he gave them his whole attention.

And he felt a strange sense of relief when, after the American's first few words, he realised that he was not being asked to consider some triviality. They

154

were actually concerned to help him. And however fantastic their notions may be, it was good to know that his burden was shared among even the most humble members of the garrison.

At first, he decided that the plan was indeed fantastic. He dismissed it mentally. But, so as to give the appearance of utter fairness, he asked questions.

It was the answers that forced him reluctantly to reconsider.

Could two men get out of the barracks unobserved?

Oui. In darkness it would not be impossible.

Could they get into the hotel?

Oui. Again it would be possible, if — as suggested — they wore Arab robes. And might they somehow force themselves between the guards and the prisoners? Might they, if they had sub-machine guns, hold the Touaregs back while a desperate rush was made from the barracks?

They would hear the shooting in the barracks. And that would be the signal. The time needed to seize the hotel? If losses were ignored — and losses would have to be ignored — it might be done in five minutes. Eight or nine minutes at the most, allowing for resistance in the street.

Monclaire drummed on the desk with his pencil.

It was a wild plan. And its main weakness lay in the fact that its success depended entirely upon only two men. Yet more than two men could not be used. Any greater number would have a proportionately smaller chance of infiltrating.

But, when all else seemed impossible, did not the wild idea sometimes succeed? Certainly. The whole history of the human race showed that . . .

Suppose he agreed . . .

Were these two legionnaires best fitted to carrying out their own plan? Or should he give the task to a couple of junior officers?

Monclaire had little difficulty in resolving that problem.

The American he knew to be courageous and quick witted. This very interview proved that. And his previous Legion record proved it, too.

And the Englishman — he had once been an officer in a British regiment. Not that that in itself was an automatic qualification, for there were many ex-officers from many armies in the ranks of the Legion. Zatov was one of them.

But Legionnaire Pete Havers had certain very desirable qualities. He lacked the innate gusto of his American friend. But he had a balancing sense of logic. A capacity for clear judgment. Like most Englishmen, he was steady under fire.

Yes, they would be an ideal pair to attempt such a desperate throw into the wheels of chance . . .

Monclaire dropped the pencil. He stood up and smiled. It was a wan smile, but then it was his first for many hours.

He said: 'I accept the plan. I will put it into operation. But neither of you needs to play the main part in it. If you prefer, I will arrange for two others to do so.'

Rex contrived to express respectful indignation while standing firmly to attention. Pete gave an almost imperceptible negative shrug of his shoulders.

'*Tres bien*. I knew it would be so. Now

157

there are many details to arrange, and we have not much time . . . '

* * *

Clong!

Five hours to midnight.

The heat in the cellar was becoming intolerable. All of them were sprawled on the floor now. All were in need of water. They had called for it, they had tried threatening for it, but none came. The only response was a muttering of Arabic abuse from the guards outside the door.

The children were making plaintive pleas. The women were trying to comfort them. The men were expressing mounting indignation.

' . . . hundreds of legionnaires within sight of the place . . . '

' . . . they don't even know a mob has seized the hotel . . . '

' . . . if I ran my exporting business the same way the Legion run their affairs I'd be . . . '

' . . . my asthma . . . '

158

8

The Cruel Lady

Monclaire said: 'I have done everything possible. I shall continue to do everything possible. Now I can only wish you good fortune.'

He tried to sound confident, but he did not feel confident, Now that the time had arrived he wondered whether he was not allowing two of his best soldiers to walk into a death trap.

Suppose the Touaregs were waiting for an attempt at infiltration? The thought had occurred to him as he watched the legionnaires putting on Arab burnouses. It had nagged him as he watched them darken their already brown faces with the potash preparation supplied by the medical officer. Was not Annice Tovak the sort of woman who would foresee such a tactic? It could be. She had proved herself a great master of the arts of the *francs-tireur*. For her, foresight would be a basic necessity.

He had thought of abandoning the entire plan.

But if he did so, what could he put in its place? Nothing. He could only wait to hear the screams at midnight. To look out when dawn came to see the mangled bodies impaled upon the barrack railings. *Non*, the plan had to go through . . .

He indicated the two Piet automatic rifles, which lay on his desk. Each was loaded with a magazine containing thirty-eight cartridges. And two spare magazines lay beside each of them.

The Piets were not a normal Legion issue. For purposes of desert warfare they — like all automatic rifles — were far too heavy on ammunition for it to be possible to equip every legionnaire with one. And, because of the short barrel and the vibration caused by the self-ejecting action, they were inaccurate at anything but the shortest range. But for such a purpose as this, they were ideal. They were easy to conceal. And they were utterly deadly.

Rex and Pete picked up the weapons.

They weighed them in their hands to get the balance. They felt strange after the long and unwieldy Lebel. There was a sharp clicking sound as they pushed over the cut-off slides and tested the trigger movements. Then they jerked free the magazines to ensure that the forcing springs were operating freely.

Satisfied, they lowered the Piets and the spare magazines into deep pockets inside the robes. There they could rest, secure and concealed. And it would be the work of a moment to bring them out.

The robes had been part of a vast conglomeration of Arabic equipment, which had assembled in the barracks over the years. The pockets had been hurriedly prepared by a legionnaire who claimed skill in such matters.

Beneath the stain, Rex's face was flushed with excitement. If Pete felt the same, he did not show it. He portrayed only the casual indifference of a man who was completely bored.

Rex said: 'Thank you, *mon officier*. If you can reach us soon after the shooting starts, we ought to be okay.'

161

Monclaire nodded.

'You can rely on that, *mes legionnaires*. Even now, two hundred men are assembled and waiting in their barrack rooms. Hold the Touaregs for ten minutes at the most, and we will be with you.'

He held out his hand. Even Pete looked slightly surprised as he shook it. It was an unusual gesture from an officer to the legionnaires.

And Monclaire added: 'Your first obstacle will be to get over the barrack railings without being seen. Fortunately there is no moon, so you ought to have no trouble . . . *bon chance*.'

They saluted awkwardly in their robes.

Then they turned to the door and were gone.

★   ★   ★

The night was a well of blackness.

Only the outline of the barrack buildings gave them their position as they crossed the northern parade ground, skirted the rifle range where Tovak had died, and made for the rear railings.

162

The railings did not come into view until they were almost upon them.

They heard a heavy crunch of feet. They belonged to the sentry. And the sentry said: 'It all clear is. But I a watch will keep.'

Rex and Pete recognised the syntax of Legionnaire Krormonn, the man from Hamburg. The plodding, conscientious Krormonn, had been ordered to help, although he had not been told exactly why. But, being a German, he accepted the order without concerning himself at all about the reason for it. Since the captain said he was to assist two legionnaires dressed as Arabs to climb over the rail — *gut*. If the captain had said he was to shoot the two legionnaires, then that would have been *gut*, also. Krormonn was a reliable soldier. But he had his limitations. Like a clock that needs frequent winding.

Rex and Pete took out their Piets and laid them just inside the rails. Pete bent almost double and Rex kneeled on his back. Then he stood upon it. From this height, but with some difficulty, Rex was able to get a hand grip round two of the top spikes. He pulled himself up until his legs were wedged on the uppermost parallel bar.

Very cautiously, he eased himself round so that he was facing towards the barracks. Then he let his legs fall free. For a moment he hung in space, then dropped to the ground. It was not a long drop, but it was a hard one because of the baked condition of the ground.

'Take it easy,' he warned Pete. 'It's a whole lot more difficult than it looks.'

Krormonn bent over to take Pete's weight. And because the German was considerably under average height, Pete found that be could not reach anywhere near the top of the rails. He did the only thing possible. He flexed his legs, and using Krormonn's back as a springboard, he jumped vertically. Krormonn uttered an obscene oath as he was forced off balance and, still holding his Lebel, crashed against the base of the rails.

It was pure ill fortune that the steel breech of Krormonn's rifle crashed against the ironwork. The resulting sound was like a ring from an untuned bell. It seemed to reverberate through the night.

Rex hissed: 'Jeeze — keep quiet! There's bound to be a few Arabs around!'

Pete had got to the top of the railings. Slowly, he followed Rex's procedure. As he dropped, Rex caught him round the waist and helped to break the impact.

They looked towards Krormonn, who was huddled on the ground.

Pete said to him impatiently: 'Push the Piets through to us . . . hurry.'

The German did not move.

Rex muttered a single and comprehensive word under his breath. He knew what had happened. Both of them knew. In his fall, Krormonn must have knocked his head against the rails — or perhaps against his rifle. Anyway, judging by his heavy breathing, he had been rendered unconscious.

And the Piets, inside the rails, were several inches out of reach. Rex, who was the taller, tested with his arm fully extended and confirmed the fact.

They gazed at each other through the

darkness. Both were in a state of baffled fury.

For one of them to go back and push the weapons through himself would be pointless, for without Krormonn's help he would not be able to make the return climb. And to return to Monclaire with a request for the help of another sentry would mean intolerable delay. And danger, too. For whoever remained lurking outside the back of the barracks would be an immediate object of curiosity to any passing Touaregs.

It was Pete who remembered the spare magazines, which were still inside their robes. He pulled one out and showed it to Rex.

Rex understood. He grabbed the long piece of hollowed metal. Holding it, he again stretched his hand inside the railings. The artificial extension of reach was more than enough. The tip of the magazine passed well beyond the Piets.

By pressing the magazine on the trigger guards, Rex was able to ease each weapon in turn towards him. Pete pulled them through the bars. And they were quickly concealed again beneath their *burnouses*.

But the incident had wasted several minutes. And it had done nothing to improve their confidence.

The agreed plan was first to strike well beyond the barracks and approach the hotel from the far side. By this means they hoped to reduce, if not eliminate, the chances of arousing suspicion. Certainly they would have little prospect of getting into the hotel if they were seen to emerge from the quiet alley at the rear of the barracks, and then make a direct and ostentatious trek towards the *Afrique's* main entrance.

First their route took them down a long and foul smelling street where Sadazi's mule and camel ostlers plied their trade. On either side were the tall doors of the stables. And from within came a discordant symphony of bestial discontent.

One stable door had been forced open, and a flickering oil lamp revealed that it was empty, save for a Bormone Arab who lay sprawled on the straw. Blood was oozing from his forehead. Rex and Pete hesitated for a moment, then moved on.

Obviously, the thieves and the thugs were taking full advantage of the chaos in the town. But there was no time to aid those who had been attacked and robbed by them.

They emerged into the European market place.

This was distinct from the market in the native quarter only because of its locality and because most of the customers were whites. The same unsavoury junk was retailed by the shrewd to the stupid.

The place was a shambles.

Flimsy wood stalls had been over-turned and smashed and their stock looted. The cobbled square was strewn with rejected foodstuffs, torn pieces of clothing material, shattered souvenirs. And once Rex and Pete stumbled over the crushed body of an Arab trader who had certainly died while trying to defend his stock.

A few gangs of Touareg youths were lurking round the place, in the hope of finding something of value. That market place was a perfect example of what always happened in any community when the forces of law are suddenly rendered helpless.

Rex and Pete had agreed to speak as little as possible. This was a basic precaution. Both had a basic smattering of several Arabic dialects, but they were not fluent enough to carry on any sustained and useful conversation. And to talk in English — unless compelled to do so — was out of the question. So they walked in silence, relieved that the marauders took no particular interest in them. The darkness — although it was now being relieved a little by the ascendant stars — was a comforting cloak.

Leaving the market place they skirted the west extremity of Rue St. Jean. Here a few of the unclaimed casualties of the morning riots still lay on the ground. Rats, long, lean and repulsive, were darting and gliding around them, making the most of the nocturnal feast.

Rex touched Pete's wrist. They stopped. They had completed a half-circle, and in the distance the stars showed up the indistinct mass of the barracks. To the right of the barracks they saw, slightly more plainly, the front of the *Hotel Afrique*.

And between them and the hotel were Touaregs.

The Touaregs had surrounded the hotel, and they were numbered now in thousands. Families of them had lit fires for comfort against the gathering winds from the Atlas Mountains, and were squatting round the flames. Groups of young warriors — many armed with scimitars and some with muskets or equally ancient pistols — were keeping an unblinking watch on the barrack gates.

Rex looked round. No one was near enough to hear, so he whispered: 'It's goin' to be one helluva job to sneak into the hotel.'

Pete shook his head.

'We'll never sneak in. Our only chance is to bluff it out. We'll have to walk in as if we owned the place.'

'Yeah? But we're bound to be stopped, and when they start asking questions we aren't goin' to sound so good.'

Pete gave a taut smile.

'My dear chap, don't be so pessimistic.

170

This was your idea. Or have you forgotten?'

Rex whispered something distinctly unflattering. But they still hesitated before attempting to move through the deep cordon.

In that moment they both knew fear. And neither was ashamed of the fact.

They knew that almost all men experienced that chilling human emotion — except, perhaps, a few fools. And it served a vital purpose. Fear was a natural brake against rash and useless action. Its only connection with cowardice lay in the fact that cowards were dominated by it, men of courage controlled and used it.

Eventually, Pete said: 'Well, we can't stand here all night . . . '

They moved into the deep circle of Arabs.

At first, it was unexpectedly easy. They edged casually through the crush and no one took any particular notice of them. There was no reason why anyone should. Their robes, their darkened skins, made them appear much the same as thousands of others there.

They were almost through the circle when they saw that a space had been cleared directly in front of the hotel entrance. It was about fifteen yards deep and twice as long. Several armed Touaregs kept the crowd from moving on to it. And a dozen other Touaregs were standing at each side of the doorway.

Obviously, they were there to ensure that no one entered or left the building without authority.

Rex glanced desperately at Pete. He decided to risk other whispered conversation, although the nearest Arabs were almost within arm's reach.

Moving his head close to Pete's, he hissed. 'We'll have to rush the place. One burst with a Piet'll fix that lot, and we ought to be able to get into the cellars before anyone knows what's happened.'

Pete did not attempt an immediate answer.

He knew that the element of surprise was their main weapon. He knew, too, that it would be madness to attempt to use it too soon. Should they work round to the back entrance and try their luck

172

there? He dismissed the alternative immediately. There would certainly be a guard there, also. And there would probably be less room for manoeuvre. So it had to be the front, or nothing.

What Pete asked himself, were the chances of bluffing the guards into letting them through? Now that he was confronted with the situation. Pete realized that they were less than nil. If either of them had spoken fluent Arabic, then a bluff might have been worth trying. But not as matters stood . . .

He heard Rex hiss: 'Did you hear what I said? We've gotta start using the Piets . . . '

Pete shook his head. He turned away and moved a few paces to a place where the mob was not so closely congested, and there was thus less chance of being overheard. Puzzled, Rex followed.

There, Pete murmured: 'We can't start a shooting match yet.'

'Oh yeah? Why not?'

'Because Monclaire is waiting for the sound of shooting — that's his signal to make a charge. The whole game would be

173

given away before we got to the prisoners
. . . as soon as the legionnaires come
pelting out of the barracks the prisoners
will be killed. Now do you understand?'

Rex understood.

Their plan was based on the premise
that somehow they would manage to get
between the prisoners and their guards
before the shooting began. If shooting
started now, they would be completely
unable to defend the Europeans, who, in
all probability, would be killed while Rex
and Pete were still trying to force their
way down to the basement.

Rex looked desperately around him.

'Okay — so what do we do?'

'Somehow we've got to divert the
attention of the Touaregs. One of us will
have to do it while the other takes the
opportunity to slip into the hotel.'

'You mean, start a fight or something?'

'Yes — something of the sort . . . now
listen. Leave the diversion to me. I'll fix it
so that for a few seconds at least, all the
Touaregs are looking away from you.
That's your chance. Take it.'

Rex stared intently at Pete.

He muttered: 'And what about you, Pete?

'I'll be all right.'

'Like hell, you will! You'll have a mob of Arabs pulling you to bits inside a couple of minutes. And you won't be able to use your gun because it'll give the alarm to the barracks too soon. No, sir. I ain't lettin' you do that.'

Pete's voice lost its normal detached calm.

'Don't talk like a hero in a Hollywood film. You've *got* to do it. So have I. Remember . . . there're twenty-two help-less people in that hotel. Some of them are women and kids. We can't stand here debating while they are done to death . . . '

'We'll have to think of something else . . . '

'There isn't anything else. We didn't expect the mob to have surrounded the whole building, and we didn't expect it to be so well guarded. So my idea's the only possible one. Now . . . '

'Listen to me, Limey! It's a punk idea! I'd have some kind of chance. But you wouldn't have any at all. I ain't doin' it, and that's final. I'll tell you what I will do. *I'll* make the disturbance and *you* can try getting into the hotel. I figure that's the way it ought to be since — '

Pete interrupted. He whispered: 'For God's sake keep your voice down!'

Rex, never very cautious, had been uttering the last few vehement sentences in above normal tones.

The warning was too late.

There was a shuffle of movement among the mob. They were making way for five Touaregs. Each was armed with a pistol. And the pistols were aimed at Rex and Pete.

Rex pushed a hand under his *burnouse*. A voice said in French: 'Leave it alone — or you'll die.' It came from behind them.

It was a woman's voice. That of Annice Tovak.

9

Special Treatment

The *Hotel Afrique* had changed. Yet it was substantially the same. It was like a new owner wearing an old coat.

The small and dusty hall with the reception desk in the corner was still there. But instead of containing a constant flow of disillusioned white people, it was now tenanted by Touaregs. They sat in the wicker chairs, and somehow expressed their arrogance even in their sitting. They looked with futile amusement at the pictures in the weeks-old French newspapers. Some of them found pleasure in ringing the aged handbell that reposed in front of a now thoroughly frightened black reception clerk.

Rex and Pete looked round in astonishment as they were half carried and half pushed into the place.

As rankers, they had never been allowed to enjoy the social amenities of the *Hotel Afrique*, So far as the Legion was concerned, it was reserved for officers only. But they were instinctively aware of the contrast.

As soon as the lounging Touaregs saw them, they gathered round them.

And they mumbled in fury as the guards pulled off the turbans and revealed first Pete's closely cropped fair hair and then Rex's equally sparse dark head.

The Touaregs watched with interest as the Piets were pulled from them.

But, because few of them understood French well, they were only puzzled and curious as Annice Tovak spoke to them.

She had a sense of drama and a sense of the fitness of things, had Annice.

In the past few hours she had discarded her western clothes and had put on purple robes. They were of fine Alleta silk, and their rich darkness contrasted with the paleness of her skin and the fairness of her hair.

She said as she recognised them: 'A

coincidence, is it not? The very legionnaires I met in the wineshop . . . the ones who helped to murder my husband!'

The latter words lashed out, like a series of cracks from a whip.

Neither Pete nor Rex answered. They were still battling with a sickness of disappointment and confusion.

She added: 'Were you alone? Or were any other legionnaires trying this stupid trick?'

They stared back at her, but still they didn't reply.

She smiled. It was that weird smile which transformed beauty into ugliness.

'I could soon find out. But it does not much matter. I thought that something of the sort might be attempted and anyone joining the crowd outside here is being watched until we are satisfied — just as you were watched. And you were not very skilful, were you? I was told that two strangers had been seen whispering together. And I arrived to hear the American shouting! No, I don't think either of you would make good secret agents!'

179

She regarded them thoughtfully. Then she said: 'You will die. You will die because of the innocent man you willingly executed.'

Rex blurted: 'There was nothing willing about it. We all felt sorry for Tovak.'

'Sorry! But you killed him just the same! How deeply do you feel sorrow? Now listen to me — for I shall give you justice. You came here because you hoped to save those prisoners. You were fools, for most of them are what? I'll tell you. They are rich, weak, flabby and cowardly. They belong to a dying social order. Their lives are not worth saving . . . '

She began to pace up and down in front of them, her slim body tensed, her eyes holding a hint of madness.

'And I shall prove what I say. When the garrison has left Sadazi, as it must, I will have you taken to the same place where my husband was executed . . .

'I shall give a rifle to each of the men who are our hostages . . .

'And I shall order them to shoot you. It will be the last condition for sparing their lives. A small additional condition . . .

'They will do it — they will do it. They are too fond of life to sacrifice it for a couple of common soldiers, even if the soldiers had risked everything to save them . . .

'Thus I shall have vengeance . . . and in the moment before you die you will know what worthless people they are, they for whom you terrorise and subjugate Morocco . . .'

Rex took in a deep breath. It expressed horror and incredulity.

Pete was the first to recover. He said dryly: 'You have a distorted sense of humour — and you're not much judge of character.'

'We shall see, and 1 know that 1 shall be proven right. These civilians when so near to safety, will certainly kill you in order to preserve their own squalid lives.'

Pete shook his head. But it was not a convincing expression of doubt. He knew that the men hostages were almost certain to represent a fairly typical cross-section of the human race. Some, no doubt, would be brave and refuse to fire. But there would be the others. The others who would gladly do her bidding.

She turned towards a Touareg who was holding the Piets. She indicated the weapons.

'And to give Monclaire something more to consider, I shall let him know immediately that you are in our hands. Your automatic rifles will be returned to him. A courtesy, which he as a Frenchman, ought to appreciate. Meanwhile, you will share a gaol next to that of your future executioners. And you will die at the same hour that he did. Eight in the morning. That . . . that gives you just a few minutes over twelve hours of life. Brood on it, legionnaires! Brood on the approaching end, even as my Kriso must have brooded . . . '

★ ★ ★

Clong!

Four hours to midnight.

The Europeans had been given a little water. It had stimulated their capacity for indignation. The Man With Asthma was being especially loquacious.

And, a few hundred yards away, Captain Monclaire was regarding a couple of Piet guns, which had been deposited on his desk.

Then he said to Lieutenant Gina, who was standing expectantly in front of him: 'Who brought them?'

'Tu el Adaa.'

'Oh, our fat friend. Is he still here?'

'*Ah oui*. He's waiting outside. He requests to speak with you.'

'Send him in.'

The repulsive vastness of Adaa made a slow advance into the office. His peculiar and staring eyes were projected at Monclaire. The featureless mass of his face was twisted into what might be taken for a smile. He started to lower himself into the other chair.

'*Stand up!*'

Monclaire rasped out the command as though on the parade ground. Adaa's body twitched under shock. He moved hastily away from the chair, some of his composure gone.

'*Capitaine*, I am a heavy man. I only . . . '

'Be quiet! You'll answer my questions, but you'll say nothing more.'

Monclaire had swiftly gained a moral ascendancy. Without the support of Annice Tovak the Arab was reverting to type.

'As you say, *capitaine*.'

There was something approaching a whine in his voice.

Monclaire asked: 'The two legionnaires — have they been hurt?'

'No . . . not yet.'

'I see. They are to be murdered, I suppose. When?'

Adaa told him. And, with some show of satisfaction, he described the proposed circumstances.

Monclaire had difficulty in controlling a desire to strangle Adaa. But he said smoothly: 'It was clearly understood that if the garrison leaves Sadazi all the civilians would be unharmed. It seems that Madame Tovak is now making extra conditions.'

Adaa gestured with fat hands. He was regaining confidence.

'She is in a position to make conditions.'

'Perhaps . . . but since I cannot trust her word in one matter, how can I trust it in others? How can I be sure that the Europeans will not be butchered whatever happens?'

'You can be sure, *capitaine*. She is a gifted woman and she had taught us much very quickly. There would be no point in killing them without reason. Would it not be a far greater victory to have forced the French out of this base without bloodshed — save for the two legionnaires? And they are of little concern. A personal matter concerning only Madame Tovak.'

Monclaire rose and walked towards the window.

He saw the lights of the hotel. Dim lights that came from oil lamps, but they seemed tragically near.

His brain was pounding — as it had pounded for hours. Like a hammer trying to break down a mighty wall. The plan, the only plan, had failed miserably. Now there was nothing left. Nothing.

Except to make a signal to Algiers. To tell them everything. To reveal the ghastly mess which misfortune had created. Misfortune? The High Command would not call it that. They would call it criminal stupidity. And both he and Jeux would probably end in a military prison, stripped of their ranks.

And the Command would have to make the decision if he sent the signal. They would have to decide whether it was to be the Legion base at Sadazi, or the lives of twenty-two civilians — many of them important foreign nationals.

Which would they decide to sacrifice? Monclaire admitted that he could not guess. It occurred to him that perhaps even the Command would shy from the issue. In fact, they probably would. It would be referred as a matter of top priority to the *Quay d'Orsay* in Paris. If that happened, the statesmen would have to think fast — very fast. They would have to decide *whether four hundred soldiers or twenty-two civilians* . . .

There was a crash within his brain. He felt a band of sweat formed at the join between his hair and his forehead. Perhaps — *oui*, perhaps the wall was crumbling. Perhaps there was yet a chance. That signal? It would not go to Algiers. *Non*.

He remained at the window for a long time. And when at last he turned towards Adaa, his face was set firm.

He said: 'If we leave Sadazi, I make it a condition that the two legionnaires be handed back here unharmed and immediately.'

'That is not possible, *capitaine*. I — I do not care. But Madame Tovak said you might say this. And she said the answer was to be no.'

'When would the Europeans be freed?'

'Three days after your departure, *capitaine*. When we are sure that you are not waiting nearby to return.'

'They will be given an escort? All the way to Oran?'

'Even so.'

Monclaire met the staring eyes of Adaa. And Adaa had to look away. Very slowly, very precisely he said: 'We shall evacuate Sadazi at midnight under these terms. But understand this. If any of those civilians is harmed, the Legion will

187

return. At whatever the cost, they will return, and the Touaregs of this town will know a terrible justice. The woman, too. I . . . I fear that I would not be among those to return. But other officers would come in my place and act in my name. Is it clear?'

Adaa had scarcely listened beyond the first few words. His round body pulsated with delight.

'You are wise, *capitaine*. 1 will go at once with your message.'

And as Adaa thudded towards the door, Monclaire said to Lieutenant Gina: 'You heard — prepare for the evacuation. And start destroying the non-movable stores and equipment.'

Gina looked horrified. But he saluted and departed.

★   ★   ★

Five minutes later Monclaire entered Colonel Jeux's bunk. Jeux was still asleep. And the place stank heavily of stale alcohol.

Monclaire snatched the empty bottle

from Jeux's hand. The action stirred him out of his stupor.

'Pull yourself together,' Monclaire said with a complete absence of military courtesy. 'I've sent for coffee. You've got to be sober to understand what I'm about to say.'

10

Preparation for Retreat

Rex and Pete were, in a comparatively trifling respect, more fortunate than the civilians in the next cellar. They had more than enough space. They had not yet suffered thirst. And they had ventilation.

Their improvised gaol was on a slightly higher elevation than the other, and at eye level a small grill was set into the wall. It was no more than four inches long and three high. But through it, it was possible to see the dim outline of the barracks and the feet of the mob that still surrounded the hotel.

They took turns to stare through it — a pointless pursuit, but one common to all who are deprived of liberty.

This had followed a prolonged attempt to make contact with the hostages next door. They had shouted. They had kicked. But the dividing wall was of thick red sandstone. It muffled every sound.

Thus the air grill became the only possible diversion in the fetid blackness.

Pete was standing there when he called to Rex. He said: 'Take a look. Things are happening at the barracks.'

Rex looked. He saw flickering flames on the front parade ground.

'Hell — have they gone crazy? Are they settin' fire to the place?'

'If you look more carefully,' Pete said, 'you'll notice that there are a number of separate fires. And they are well away from the building.'

'Then what are they doing? Just keeping themselves warm?'

'It seems to me as though they are burning the equipment.'

Rex gave a long whistle.

'Y'mean . . . '

'Exactly. Equipment isn't destroyed for fun, old man. I mean that the garrison is going.'

They were silent for a few moments, both peering anxiously. Then they heard a series of faint popping sounds, which probably came from the vicinity of the rifle range.

'Now what?' Rex asked. 'Are they shooting at each other?'

'Not quite. They'll be burning the small arms ammunition. There's no danger if the slugs are first pulled out of the cartridge casings. That's what they'll have done.'

'It sure looks like they're not goin' to leave much for the Arabs to collect.'

'Yes,' Pete said. 'It does. And I fancy we'll get a good view of the destruction when we're taken to the range in the morning.'

* * *

Annice Tovak saw the flames and heard the weak explosions from a room she had commandeered in the hotel. She ran the point of her tongue round her rich lips.

And she said to Adaa, who was at her side: 'This, my fat friend, is memorable! Those are the fires of victory that colour the air!'

Adaa raised a hand in emphatic agreement.

Then she added with sudden venom:

'Do you now see that nothing is impossible? Do you not understand that the power of the old tyrannies can be destroyed if one has determination enough? Look, my friend. Those fires will consume an empire. When the story of Sadazi is told, the oppressed peoples of all Africa will rise against their masters. And I — I, Annice Tovak — will lead them wherever they need me. I will teach them to strike without fear and without pity, as I learned to do against those who oppressed my own people in Europe.'

★ ★ ★

Sergeant Zatov raised a fist to the heavens as though demanding divine intervention. Then he glared at Lieutenant Gina.

'Mon officier!'

It was more of a command than a preliminary statement of respect.

Gina, who was supervising the fires, looked faintly shocked.

'You wish to speak to me? Then don't do so in that tone of voice.'

Gina flushed as he spoke. He could never hand out a reprimand without sounding like a nervous young schoolmaster. He was aware of the fact and it embarrassed him. In the privacy of his bunk he had tried modelling his voice on that of Monclaire. Tried to master that tone of quiet finality. But it would never come. Gina knew that his voice was too thin. And his experience too brief. He was aware, as he looked up at Zatov, that the monstrous N.C.O. thought him ridiculous.

Zatov was saying: 'I wish to ask, *mon officier*, are these all the stores that are to be destroyed?'

'Er — *oui*. Plus the small arms ammunition.'

'But, *mon officier*, this is only spare bedding material. And only a few boxes of the ammunition are being burned. Are we to leave all the rest for those . . . ?'

He was surprised to see that Gina was smiling at him. A nervous, immature smile. But it was genuine.

A thought struck Zatov. He smiled, too.

'Ah, *officier*, is it that we are to return soon — ?'

Gina nodded.

'*Oui*. We are to return. Now find Captain Monclaire. He wants to speak to you.'

11

The Vultures of Sadazi

Monclaire glanced at his watch. Twenty minutes past eleven. He pulled on his greatcoat and buttoned it carefully. Then he strapped his pistol belt over it. His *kepi* followed. He glanced at his reflection in the office window. It was an inadequate reflection. He looked vaguely transparent. But it sufficed to show that each detail of his dress was correct. He picked up his cane and took a last look round.

The office seemed much the same as usual. But there was not much about it that could be changed. The only furniture was the desk, a couple of chairs, and the filing cabinet. That filing cabinet was now empty and the drawers open. That was the only real departure from normal. The Touaregs would find little to interest them there.

He strode out, leaving the door

unlocked. There was no point in inviting a mob to smash it open.

A single oil lamp flickered in the corridor. Its light created shadows that were deep and ominous. Monclaire paused to blow it out.

Then he strode through the double doors, down the six wide steps, and on to the front parade ground.

A slight and pallid figure emerged from the gloom. It was Lieutenant Gina.

Gina came carefully to attention and saluted. When the courtesy had been returned, Gina said: 'The garrison's ready for inspection, *capitaine*.'

'*Merci, mon lieutenant*.'

They moved towards the flank of the front file. A *sous lieutenant* called a command. The file made a single movement, then clicked into rigidity.

There seemed to be a great many of them. Viewed from Monclaire's angle, the men merged into the night. It was impossible to see more than a quarter of the way along the column.

And Monclaire — who liked finding similes — thought that, in full marching order, they looked like young camels. The valises on their backs — each supporting a tent sheet and a blanket — gave the appearance of small humps.

He began the inspection. He did it thoroughly, pausing occasionally to adjust a legionnaire's shoulder strap or examine some other part of the equipment for cleanliness.

He thought: 'They are cursing me for doing this . . . they think I am mad to hold an inspection in the middle of the night . . . but we are not scampering out of Sadazi like a rabble . . . we shall march away as soldiers of France . . .'

When he had inspected most of the third and last file he became aware of a sudden and familiar rumbling of voices. It came from outside the railings. He glanced at Gina.

'It seems,' Monclaire said, 'that we are to be given a hearty send off.'

Gina wanted to say something equally casual, equally mature and composed. He made a turbulent excavation of his vocabulary. But all he could produce was, '*Ah oui, capitaine,*' plus a thin laugh. He was furious with himself.

When he had looked at the last legionnaire, Monclaire paused to glance towards the railings. Many of the mob were carrying tallow lamps and the light from them showed up a heaving concourse. They were struggling for the best positions to see the last of the Legion. And already they were screaming abuse at the garrison.

Gina hesitated, then said vehemently: *'Canaille!'*

Monclaire shook his head.

'*Non*, they are not that. They are not a true rabble. They have merely fallen under the spell of bad arguments and lies. Backward peoples, wherever you may find them, are always the easiest material for the unscrupulous. It is too easy. They promise them a freedom that they could not use. They mouth the phrases of democracy to peoples who cannot read or write. And to what purpose? In the end the liberators become the new governors — and often far harsher ones than those they have deposed. And peoples such as we see out there are taught to sing the songs of freedom even as the tyrant's whip lashes their backs ... *Non, mon ami*, they, the masses, are not to blame. They are not *canaille*. You will find the true *canaille* among the people like Madame Tovak. People who use superior intelligence deliberately to mislead the less fortunate.'

Gina said diffidently: 'But she may be exceptional, *capitaine*. She has cause to hate us.'

'It only makes it worse. She has used these people as an instrument of her own grudge. But the background was there all the time. Do you remember where she comes from?'

'*Oui*. Czechoslovakia.'

'Exactly. And she could not have left there without the approval of her government. *Mon ami* ... I feel sure that she came here knowing that her husband could not leave the Legion until he had served his five years. She intended to use that as a means of causing as much trouble for us as possible. Then she found he was dead. She knew grief, *oui*. But she also saw a great opportunity. She is clever, is Madame Tovak. She has used her opportunity well.'

Monclaire broke off, as though realising that he might have said too much. He was not in the habit of conveying his private views to officers while on parade. But, on balance, he was glad he had spoken thus to Gina. The mere act of articulation had clarified points that had been dormant and confused in his mind.

He had no doubt now that Annice Tovak was much more than a woman rendered crazed with shock and sorrow. Those emotions — although genuine enough — only stimulated and aided her in the work she had undertaken.

But now a more immediate problem had to be faced — the orderly evacuation of Sadazi.

He returned to the front of the file by way of the right flank. There the horse transport was assembled. This consisted of the mobile kitchen — smelling faintly of countless forgotten *soupe* stews — and the Red Cross wagon. The rear curtains of this were slightly apart. Through the aperture Colonel Jeux's braided cap could be clearly seen.

In fact, it seemed as though the cap might fall out when the wagon moved. But Monclaire ignored the possible loss. He let it remain there on the edge of the floor, with a brandy bottle to keep it company.

Satisfied, Monclaire tucked his cane under his left arm and gave an order. It was repeated by Zatov, as the senior N.C.O. The three files made a left turn from the *repos* position.

'*Gare a vous!*'

They turned to attention. Lebels were sloped. '*Avant! Par droit . . .* '

The sudden rhythm of many marching feet was startling. The boots clashed hollowly and starkly on the hard surface, drowning for the moment the shouting of the Arabs.

The long column made a wheel towards the open gates. There the small remaining guard presented arms, then fell in at the rear of the horse transport.

The retreat had begun.

And as Monclaire led them out, chaos broke loose among the mob. The loathing of years found expression in a roar of obscenities. Fists and scimitars were brandished, a few stones were thrown.

The noise was like that of an unrelenting hurricane.

But not all the Arabs showed hate. Here and there were tongues that did not accuse, fists that did not threaten.

And one of those was an ancient crone. She had withered with the years, and now she was dry and ugly, like an old twig. But fires had been lit in her dim and rheumy eyes. Her quavering voice trembled above the tumult.

'Oh, you foolish ones,' she called to those who pressed around her. 'You children of evil . . . '

Some of the mob, realising that she was not declaiming the soldiers, became quiet and listened.

'You embrace your own damnation,' she told them. 'I — I who am older than any of you, can tell of the days before the French came among us! I can tell of the time when no Arab of the alleys was safe from the slave traders . . . when our lives could be taken to give sport to a sheikh! But the French ended such things, I tell you! When the French came to Morocco, the weak were protected from the strong and all men found justice . . .

'Now — now you drive away the shield that has guarded you and you find joy in your own future sorrows . . . '

Her old voice faded and cracked. There was laughter among the mob. Malicious laughter. Then they turned again to the pleasure of jeering at the departing Legion.

★   ★   ★

Clong!

Midnight.

Most of the hostages were sleeping in hot and hard discomfort. But a few were awake.

' . . . what's that row going on outside . . . ?'

' . . . sounds like some native festival . . . '

' . . . perhaps they're going to let us out of here . . . '

' . . . we've got to be released sometime. I mean, even the Legion can't remain in ignorance of this outrage forever . . . '

' . . . y'know, I think the garrison's had the infernal cheek to go on a route march. I'm sure I heard marching feet . . . '

' . . . and they gave me a book in the tourist office. It said something about visiting a real Foreign Legion base in comfort . . . '

'I might as well die now and be finished with it. With my asthma, I'll never be normal again . . . '

★   ★   ★

Annice Tovak adjusted the unfamiliar robes. She found the garments uncomfortable and slightly ridiculous. But it had been a good decision to wear them. She must identify herself as closely as possible with the outward characteristics of the people. If the ordinary Touareg women did not wear such rich robes as hers, Annice did not worry.

Some distinction was necessary for a leader.

She continued to gaze out of the window as the column marched past.

Here, she decided, was her greatest accomplishment. She had caused dissension and violence in many parts of Europe — but this, her first visit to Africa, had produced the supreme result. It had been a masterstroke to send her to Sadazi when it was discovered that Kriso was stationed there in the Legion.

For then two motions were combined into an irresistible whole — her loyalty to the Cause and her love for her husband. But the Cause came first.

Perhaps . . . yes, perhaps it was even worth losing Kriso for such a victory as this.

Not, she told herself, that Kriso would have seen it that way. He had always been weak, timid.

It was that which made him appeal to her. She was strong, and she liked to give him the protection of that strength. It was a pity, but she had never met a man who could dominate her, or outwit her

Never . . . unless . . .

There was that damned Frenchman . . . Monclaire . . .

He had been hard to break. He had

206

courage, but not much cunning. That had been Monclaire's weakness.

And now, there he was.

Marching at the head of the retreating garrison. Defeated without a shot being fired.

She turned to Adaa.

'Send for the two legionnaires. I want them to see this,' she said.

She waited impatiently, for she did not want them to miss the spectacle. Her face was glowing with anticipation when four armed Touaregs escorted Rex and Pete into the room. She noted that their wrists had been bound. That was good. She knew the type. They were capable of attempting anything.

'Come here,' she said, 'and look . . . '

Rex and Pete were pushed towards the window. She watched their faces as they stared down at the long column and at the jeering, jostling mob.

Rex compressed his lips and his eyes narrowed. He whispered a lurid Brooklyn deprecation. But Pete offered no reaction. His features remained bland, as though he were taking a polite interest in a rather tedious ceremonial parade.

She said: 'Look on it well! They are going. And you are alone. They have deserted you, for the sake of a handful of worthless civilians — the civilians who will slay you within a few hours.'

Pete slowly turned his head towards her.

He said: 'Madame, you're much too melodramatic. Frankly, we find you rather a bore.'

Like many Englishmen of his background, Pete could be supremely insulting. He emphasised that fact as he added: 'I believe that condemned men are usually granted a last request. I'll make mine now. I want you to take that preposterous robe off. It's not at all impressive, I assure you. In fact, you look as if you're about to take a bath.'

For a moment it seemed as though she was going to strike him. Her small round breasts were heaving visibly as she fought to control herself.

She said with an effort: 'You are a legionnaire, eh? But I think you are also an English *aristo*. Well, understand this — we could easily change that insolent

208

tongue of yours. We could reduce you to what you really are — a snivelling, decadent wretch. But I think it is not worthwhile to bother now. I will be there to see you whine for mercy when you face the rifles in the morning.'

She looked again out of the window. The column had almost passed. The rear end, with the horse transport, was coming into view. She glared at it for a moment, then she smiled cruelly and pointed to the Red Cross wagon.

'See . . . There is a symbol before your eyes! A symbol of the decadence of which I spoke! There is your commandant. Oh, I have heard of him. Heard that he is forever soaked in brandy. And now, look! He cannot even lead his men in their final shame. He is helpless with drink . . . '

She broke into an ugly laugh, a finger still pointing to the wagon.

There Rex and Pete saw the cap that could only belong to Colonel Jeux. And they glimpsed, too, a bottle inside the awning.

They turned away, her laughter still in their ears.

And they heard her say to Adaa: 'Put a strong guard on the barracks. The place will be occupied properly in the morning. It is valuable and I do not want to see it torn to pieces.'

As Adaa — who had become remarkably docile — rolled weightily away, Annice said to Rex and Pete: 'There is one other formality. The civilians know little of what has been happening. They do not even know why they have been held captive. But now I am going to tell them. And I am going to tell the men that they will have to shoot you — if they wish to live. Come — you are going to witness the interview . . . '

She moved out of the door. Rex and Pete were pushed after her.

Lamps were produced by the Touareg guards as they approached the cellar. When the door was unlocked their light revealed a sprawling conglomeration of humanity.

The men, who had been talking, stared curiously at Annice and furiously at the Touaregs. Then, seeing Rex and Pete, their faces momentarily cleared. They were about to express relief at seeing the Legion — until they saw that their hands were bound. Then they gaped in futile astonishment.

Annice waited until all were fully awake. She seemed oblivious of the heat and the rancid atmosphere of the place. She stood very still. And she paid no attention when several of the men started to demand an explanation.

Then, when the men had realised the uselessness of talking, she began to speak. She did so quietly, but vibrantly. The hostages gazed at her as if she were an uncanny phenomenon. At first their features reflected disgusted disbelief as she told them that the garrison had gone — and why. But, as one cogent sentence followed another, their demeanour portrayed sickly horror.

Then, turning specifically to the men, she said: 'These two legionnaires came here in the hope of liberating you. They will confirm all that I have said. Ask them.'

There was an uneasy silence. Then a little man who had forgotten to replace his dentures hissed: 'Well — is it true?'

His tones contained an indirect plea. He wanted to hear that it was not so. That it was all some outrageous mistake.

Rex hesitated. There seemed no point in avoiding the issue. He nodded.

'Yeah — it's right enough! The garrison has quit so as to save your lives.'

'But even now — what guarantee have we that we'll not be done to death?'

'None,' Rex told him reluctantly. 'But you have a good chance now. You would have faced certain death if the garrison had stayed.'

Annice nodded. She was enjoying the interview, and she was well satisfied with its progress.

She said: 'But the American has not told you of the one final condition for sparing your lives. Since he is sensitive about it, I will do so. You, the men here, will shoot them in the Legion barracks at eight o'clock this morning!'

By now the hostages were beyond any capacity for incredulity. They absorbed the statement with the sluggish reluctance of a waterlogged sponge. Then, after several seconds, they reacted.

An important and well-nourished look-ing man who was on some obscure committee of the United Nations, pushed his way forward.

He said: 'I can only think, *madame*, that you are a criminal lunatic. But in any case, you will be severely punished for this burlesque. All of us here are either tourists or residents in Sadazi. We are not murderers. And certainly we would not murder two soldiers who attempted to get us out of this place.'

'As you wish. You may keep your principles intact and lose your life, if you feel that way. But you and the others will each be given a rifle and one round of ammunition. At a signal, you will be ordered to fire at the legionnaires. Those of you who do not do so will die quite painfully.'

The Man With Asthma had been coughing into a handkerckief. He had no hair and he blinked through thick glasses.

'I refuse! I won't do it!'

'We shall see. I mentioned a painful death. Perhaps you would like to know the details. I think one of the guards will demonstrate to you.'

She gestured, and a Touareg came forward. He drew a short blade from under his *burnous*. The cruel steel glittered as he advanced. He placed a hand on the man's shoulder so as to hold him firm. Then, with the extreme point of the blade, he drew a design over the lower part of his abdomen. The knife scarcely harmed the clothing. But the meaning was revoltingly clear. One of the women screamed. Others muttered threats. But Annice was unperturbed.

'Now,' she asked, 'do you understand?'

The Man With Asthma showed all the symptoms of extreme fear. His eyes were wild, his jaw slack. Sweat oozed down his face and even out of the top of his bare scalp. He was a comfortable man. Except for his chest affliction, he had probably never known a moment's hardship in his life until now.

But deep down in him there was some of the stuff of which greatness is made.

He blurted back: 'I don't care — you can cut me to pieces. I still won't do it . . .'

A woman rushed to him and put her arms round his neck. She was short and fat. They made an unlovely pair. But there was no doubt of the affection which existed between them. She wept, and he tried to console her with meaningless mumblings.

Annice watched. Then she shrugged her shoulders. She had obviously come to a decision.

She said: 'I don't want to see any exhibitions of mock heroism when the time comes for the execution I have planned. And so I can be sure that you will all be a little more docile, I am going to have our friend killed now — in front of you.'

The woman screamed as a Touareg dragged her away. The Touareg with the knife smiled and tested the blade on his brown hand. The Man With Asthma blinked several times in rapid succession, as though trying to wake from a nightmare. But he did not cringe or cower away.

It was Pete who halted the horror. He said to Annice: 'Let me talk to them . . .

I think I can persuade them not to be silly.'

She looked surprised. But she nodded.

'Very well. If you think you can give courage to your own executioners, do so.'

Pete paused to collect his thoughts and to still the emotions he would never have revealed. Then he said: 'I want you to know that you will gain nothing by refusing to shoot us. We would die in any case. You must do as she says, and then I think your lives will be preserved.'

The Man With Asthma wheezed dramatically.

'We can't do it — there are limits!'

Pete smiled at him. It was a friendly smile.

'You can do it, and you must. If you die you leave your families alone in this place. When we die, we leave nothing and no one. My friend and I came here knowing the risk. We are paid to take risks. If you aim well and true when the time comes, we'll have no cause to complain.'

Rex nodded assent.

Then they looked at each other — the hostages and the two legionnaires. The

Man With Asthma said: 'I've — I've never really done anything worth while since the day I was born. I've had things too easy. I — I thought that . . . '

Pete broke in gently.

'I know how you feel. But what you say is not true. You have done something worthwhile. A few seconds ago you were faced with a terrible death and you did not run away . . . You may never have worn a uniform sir, but you would be a good soldier in any army.'

The Man With Asthma was near to tears. But he straightened his flabby shoulders. He pulled in his paunch. And he saluted with the wrong hand as Rex and Pete were pushed out of the cellar.

* * *

The staff officers at Algiers had dined well and wined well. In the mess there was an atmosphere of mellow content. Of satisfaction with the past and confidence in the future.

They had been discussing informally the difficulties of guarding the new oil lines in places where they ran through hostile territory. The Tutana area, of course, was a special problem. Interesting, too. Full of unusual strategical and tactical considerations. And, although it was now past midnight, they were loath to let the matter drop.

At the General's suggestion they repaired to the map room.

And there, the recently promoted General Panton, formerly commandant at Dini Sadazi, switched on the wall lights. They illuminated the mile-to-the-inch scale plan of North Morocco. The less elevated staff officers gathered round as the General picked up a cane and prepared to explain.

'In Sadazi, gentlemen, we have the advantage of a secure and well equipped forward base,' he announced. 'A glance at the map . . . ' — there was an agonising pause while he searched, desperately for Sadazi and an audible sigh of relief when the pointer alighted on the name — ' . . . a glance will show us that any hostility from the Touaregs can be promptly dealt with by the garrison there . . . '

He cleared his throat and paused heavily. His satellites stared raptly at his flaccid face, as though hoping that even his features might project some jewels of military wisdom.

' . . . Indeed, as you know, gentlemen, a column leaves from Sadazi for Tutana within a few hours. The orders went to Colonel Jeux yesterday, and we may rely on him to put them into prompt and efficient effect . . . '

The fruity voice went on, and on — and still on.

But when at last General Panton was in his room, he permitted himself his nightly luxury. He enacted an imaginary scene in which he, General Panton, played a leading and heroic part.

He was being called into the presence of the President of France.

Panton stood to attention before his bed while listening to a non-existent voice congratulating him on the manner in which he had secured the oil lines.

Monsieur le President said: 'By your skilful dispositions and your constant inspiration to those serving under you,

you have brought glory to France and security to the Western world.'

To Panton, that voice was real. It was not his own bed he was staring at. It was a gilded chair on a dais in which sat the supreme head of State.

And Panton replied aloud: 'Your Excellency is more than kind. It is more than a poor soldier deserves.'

He blushed modestly. Then his right hand opened and closed, as if threatened by palsy. But, to Panton's vivid imagination, the motion signified that he was receiving the baton of a Marshal of France.

He saluted the empty bed. He acknowledged the polite applause of the glittering assembly.

Then he undressed, put on his pyjamas, and retired for the night.

12

Counter-Stroke

Dawn.

Monclaire rubbed a hand over his haggard and unshaven face. He looked over the undulations of red sand. Beyond the clusters of cactus and camel-thorn. He tried to pierce the impossible distance, the five miles that lay between where he and his men had bivouacked and Dini Sadazi.

If only he could see what was happening there . . .

Lieutenant Gina came up to him, rubbing his eyes. Gina, it seemed, had been able to get some sleep in the three hours since they had made camp. In that respect he was more fortunate than Monclaire, who had waited and wondered through the dark and lonely hours.

Gina said nervously: 'I shouldn't worry too much, *capitaine*.'

Monclaire scowled at him.

'I really don't need your fatuous attempts at consolation,' he said sharply.

Gina flushed a rich pink, and Monclaire immediately regretted the unjustified reprimand.

'Forgive me,' he said. 'I'm tired. And I don't like this. Never before have I had to wait like this without being able to do anything. It does not seem natural. And with so much in the balance . . . '

He ended with a Gallic gesture of the hands.

Gina glanced towards the long, orderly lines of sleeping men and the few sentries who walked between them.

'Shall we strike camp?' he asked. 'It's nearly seven o'clock.'

'*Oui*. We start to march exactly on the hour. The timing must be precisely correct.'

'It will be correct,' Gina said, in the sure knowledge that Monclaire would make it so.

★ ★ ★

Pete looked at his watch. It was a British Army issue, big and accurate. One of his few souvenirs of happier days.

'Nearly seven o'clock,' he said.

Rex, who was sitting propped against the wall, grunted. His brow was furrowed.

He said: 'Y'know, I just can't understand Monclaire quitting the town like that. I know there was nothing else he could do — maybe. But just the same, it isn't like him. That guy just isn't the sort who quits.'

'Not in the ordinary way, he isn't. But he's never faced a situation like this before, and neither has anyone else.'

'Maybe he plans on making a surprise return to Sadazi.'

'Perhaps, but I don't think that would do much good. If he returns within three days the Europeans will be killed. And if he returns after three days you can bet the Touaregs will have got a tight grip on this place. It'd need a full-scale war to get them out. And our prestige would never be the same.'

Rex said: 'Y'know — I've just been thinking . . . it's only forty-eight hours

223

ago since we were preparing to shoot Tovak . . . '

'The same thought has been on my mind, old chap. There's no doubt that that bitch is a master of the dramatic twist. And she's accomplished a devil of a lot in those two days.'

'Yeah . . . but I guess she'd be okay if she wasn't so darned crazy . . . '

'You're susceptible, Rex. Okay for what?'

'Well . . . Say, I'm getting scared.'

'And I. And I think I'm going to be a lot more scared before long. The idea of being executed by a bunch of civilians who've never held a rifle before does not appeal to me.'

'Maybe they'll miss us altogether.'

'In that case they'll probably be told to keep trying. We'll most likely look like pepper pots before we kick the bucket.'

'That's right, Pete, cheer me up!'

They scrounged in their tunics for cigarette stubs. Rex found one. He divided it and they smoked, their hands shaking.

★   ★   ★

224

Twelve minutes to eight!

God, no! It was eleven minutes to eight. The clock hand had just moved.

Rex, peering through the ventilation grille, licked his dry lips with an equally dry tongue. He said to Pete: 'It won't be long now, bud.'

They heard the pad of sandalled feet in the corridor outside. They went past their own door. They stopped at the next cellar.

There was a faint scuffle of movement. Then the sound of hard shoes walking slowly on stone.

Pete joined Rex at the grille.

The mob outside seemed to have diminished since night. Probably many of the Arabs had retired exhausted after the long hours of triumph and hysteria. There seemed to be only a few hundred gathered outside the main gates of the barracks. And most of them were quiet, almost jaded, as if they had exhausted their capacity for emotion. The execution, it seemed, was not attracting much attention.

And it seemed also that it was to be a restricted affair. None of the mob was being allowed into the barracks. A dozen Touareg guards were standing there, keeping all potential spectators away.

Pete was about to comment on this when they saw the execution squad.

It consisted of eight men hostages. Precisely the same number that had shot Legionnaire Tovak. They shambled in a nervous and ungainly group towards the gates, shepherded by warriors. The Man With Asthma was at the back. He walked in a dazed way, as though in his sleep.

Then the door of their cellar was unlocked and pushed open. Annice Tovak stood in the entrance. Her face was pale. The normal richness of her lips had been compressed into a couple of horizontal lines.

She said: 'You do not look so happy, my friends! You are suffering I think. That is good. I hope you are suffering as much as my Kriso suffered two days ago!'

They did not answer because they could not trust their voices.

She nodded to the guards, who gripped their arms and pushed them out of the cellar.

At first they blinked in the sudden sunlight as they crossed towards the barracks. A few Arabs spat upon them. Others jeered and cursed. But the same general apathy that they had noticed earlier, prevailed. The population had had a surfeit of excitement.

They passed through the gates.

Pete told himself: 'This is a nightmare. It just can't be true.'

And Rex thought: 'I must have been a bad guy somewhere back to have deserved this . . . ' The insolent and semi-barbaric Touareg warriors in place of the immaculate Legion sentries . . . A few Arabs of high degree walking the parade ground, which had been the domain of the Legion . . . it twisted and corrupted the imagination.

They walked over the parade ground that skirted the main buildings of the barracks. Then they were at the rifle range. At the place where executions were always held.

The preparations had been made most carefully.

The stake at which Tovak had stood

was still there, its wood chipped by bullets. But another stake had been erected at its side. They were separated by less than four inches.

Annice Tovak came up to them. She was smiling. It was the evil smile.

She said softly, almost caressingly: 'It has come, my friends! Is there anything I can say to make it easier for you? Any words of comfort I can offer?'

It was the mockery of a diseased and unbalanced mind. They ignored it so far as they could. But the gentle mockery continued: 'Look at the big clock! Look at it even as my Kriso must have looked at it in his last moments. It says four minutes to eight. You have four minutes to live, for when it strikes I shall give the order to your executioners. Look at them! Look at the men you tried to save! They cannot kill you fast enough. Their one concern is for their own bloated lives.'

They looked. A Touareg was putting a single shot into each of eight aged muzzle-loading guns. He handed a loaded gun to each of the men. Behind the execution squad stood a dozen armed

Touaregs there, no doubt, to quell any last moment revulsion or rebellion.

They noticed the Man With Asthma. His hand was trembling as though stricken with convulsion as he took his gun.

Pete murmured to Rex: 'That lot'll never hit us if they go on trying all day.'

But Annice overheard. She said: 'That is not true. I have told them that they will be allowed three rounds in which to kill you. If they fail in that time, my undertaking to preserve their lives will be void. I think you will find that their aim is good!'

A Touareg handed her two pieces of black cloth. She took them, then she inspected them doubtfully.

'I had wondered,' she said, 'whether to use these. Frankly, I would far rather see your eyes — see the horror in them the moment before you die. But I am conscientious. I was trained to be thus. I want to bring your execution into line as far as possible with that of my husband. I want as many details as possible to be the same. So you will be blindfold.'

She gave an order and they were pushed to the stakes. They did not resist. There would have been no point in doing so. Their hands and feet were lashed to the wood. She walked behind them. First she wrapped a piece of black cloth over Pete's eyes, making a viciously tight knot. Rex was next. They heard her say: 'Two minutes to eight. You have that time to live. In another minute you shall hear me giving the orders to your bloated executioners . . .'

★ ★ ★

Colonel Jeux felt longingly at the flask in his hip pocket. It was half-full — or half-empty, depending on one's point of view — with brandy. Not a top-level brandy. Not a *Dubouche* or even a *Courvausiare*. Such would be spoiled in a flask. But, nonetheless, it was a solidly stimulating drink. And he wanted some of it badly. His head felt like an inflated pumpkin. But he resisted the temptation. Only two more minutes and he would have other things to think about.

If he *could* think . . .

That was the danger. What if, even in this terrible moment, his brain refused to function?

It was a ghastly thought. Perhaps just one pull would help . . . *Mais non.* He had promised Monclaire. He would keep that promise.

But that infernal ticking was driving him mad. It ate into the brain. He had never realised how much noise the clock at Sadazi made. No one could possibly realise it, unless they spent hours closeted inside the clock tower with fifty legionnaires.

Still, Jeux thought, it must be just as bad for his men. They all looked tense after the long spell of waiting.

They were specially selected, those fifty legionnaires. Not a freshly trained recruit among them. Each was battle hardened, each a tested veteran. And each of them looked it, as they crouched around gripping their specially issued Piet guns.

It had, Jeux conceded, been a good idea of Monclaire's. A stroke of genius, in fact. He had realised that the Arabs would not be able to check upon whether the *whole* of the garrison left Sadazi. So why not leave a small, highly efficient group behind? And conceal them until the moment when there was the best chance of rescuing both the hostages and the two legionnaires. The clock tower was the best place to hide. The moment before the hideous execution was best in which to strike. And, strangely enough, Monclaire had suggested that he, Jeux, was the best man to lead the operation. Why? Because it would be so easy to let the Arabs and that woman believe that he was drunk and helpless in the first-aid wagon.

It had not been very flattering, of course. But Jeux was dispassionate enough to know that he had not done much recently to justify flattery.

It was one minute to eight. He could see that by the inside reflection of the clock hands. He had been looking vertically upwards almost every other second for the last ten minutes. Thank heaven it was not over. The time had come.

Jeux stood up. He drew out his pistol. The legionnaires saw him do it. They did not need any further orders. They cocked the pins of their Piets. They sucked their lips. Those tough, villainous looking fighting men were already savouring the delights of battle. Jeux absorbed some of their confidence.

'*Avant!*' he shouted.

For a fraction of a moment he was surprised by his own voice. It was not rusty any more. It was strong. It had a ring to it . . .

His command was taken up by the men.

'*Avant . . .* '

They stormed down the narrow, circular stairs behind Jeux. They burst out on to the parade ground.

The clock still showed half a minute to eight when they reached the perimeter of the rifle range. Then the air was torn by the ghastly clatter of the Piets.

But the first casualty was not caused by a Legion Piet.

It was caused by an eighty-year-old Beloni musket. A muzzle loader. And it was fired by the Man With Asthma.

With it he sent an uncovered lead

bullet across twenty yards of space until it ended in the chest of Annice Tovak.

The slug, utterly unexpected, knocked her sideways as if she had received a blow on the shoulder. Then she spun slowly and gracefully round, clutching the place between her breasts.

There was an oath on her lips when she died.

★ ★ ★

One of Jeux's main worries had been whether he could capture and hold the barracks until Monclaire returned. His arrival was timed for thirty minutes past eight.

Jeux need not have felt any concern.

The recapture of the barracks was no problem at all, for the Touaregs had not yet properly occupied it. The later resistance was negligible. The Touaregs were shocked, humiliated, dazed and leaderless.

The rest of the garrison returned to a very quiet and a very law-abiding Dini Sadazi.

★ ★ ★

At nine o'clock a bugle sounded. Its thin notes were strangely lovely on the morning air. And at the same time the Tricolour went up on the flag mast.

Monclaire was watching from Jeux's room. His face was lined and weary. But his eyes were bright.

'I've kept my word,' he whispered to himself. 'I swore that the civilians would not die. And I swore that the Tricolour would rise again ... '

Jeux, who was standing at his side, said: *'Pardon?'*

But Monclaire pretended not to hear.

★ ★ ★

At eleven o'clock ...

Monclaire's company left for the Tutana region. The *capitaine* smiled at Rex and Pete as he inspected them before departure.

'You all right, *mes legionnaires?*'

'*Oui, capitaine.*'

'Fit to march?'

235

'*Oui, capitaine.*'

'It has been quite an experience . . . '

★ ★ ★

At noon . . .

General Panton was most annoyed. He held a radio cipher slip. He glared at it. Then he turned to his aide.

'This,' he declared, 'is intolerable. The message here says that the patrol was delayed by some three hours before departing for Tutana. They say there were some minor civil disturbances which have now been settled. *Dieu!* What nonsense! Can't Jeux deal with a noisy rabble without having to call on the entire garrison? It wouldn't have happened in my day . . . '

THE END

We do hope that you have enjoyed reading this large print book.

Did you know that all of our titles are available for purchase?

We publish a wide range of high quality large print books including:
Romances, Mysteries, Classics
General Fiction
Non Fiction and Westerns

Special interest titles available in large print are:
The Little Oxford Dictionary
Music Book, Song Book
Hymn Book, Service Book

Also available from us courtesy of Oxford University Press:
Young Readers' Dictionary
(large print edition)
Young Readers' Thesaurus
(large print edition)

For further information or a free brochure, please contact us at:
Ulverscroft Large Print Books Ltd.,
The Green, Bradgate Road, Anstey,
Leicester, LE7 7FU, England.
Tel: (00 44) **0116 236 4325**
Fax: (00 44) **0116 234 0205**

Other titles in the
Linford Mystery Library:

TO DREAM AGAIN

E. C. Tubb

Ralph Mancini, an officer in the United Nations Law Enforcement Agency, is dedicated to the world-wide War on Drugs. A new drug is developed, giving a uniquely effective 'trip', whereby people become God-like beings and they experience 'heaven'. The next trip is their only priority — whatever the cost. Ralph and Inspector Frere follow a tangled trail of murder, seeking the source of the peril — but will they be too late to stop it spreading across the world?

SPIDER MORGAN'S SECRET

John Russell Fearn

When the little crook, Spider Morgan, bursts into Victoria Lincoln's office, he's being followed — and his life is in danger. She lets him hide in her office strongroom and soon two bogus police officials pay a call. They question Victoria about Spider, but she sends them on their way. The next day she learns that Morgan has been beaten senseless and left in a coma. Then after her office is burgled — Victoria and her staff are being followed . . .

THE GOLDEN HORNS

John Burke

In wartime Denmark, Martin Slade was a saboteur, then, in post-war Europe — a smuggler. Now, burying his past — he's a respectable journalist — going back to Denmark to cover a music festival. When he's approached by his old flame, Birgitte Holtesen, he spurns her and she, instead, ensnares an English musician, Sean Clifford. Returning home to England, Martin is attacked in his flat, which has been ransacked. Then he learns that Clifford has been murdered — and his body horribly mutilated . . .